Lulu vs. Love

Lulu vs. Love

TRICIA SPRINGSTUBB

ILLUSTRATED BY JILL KASTNER

Delacorte Press

Published by
Delacorte Press
Bantam Doubleday Dell Publishing Group, Inc.
666 Fifth Avenue
New York, New York 10103

Library of Congress Cataloging in Publication Data

Springstubb, Tricia.
    Lulu vs. Love / by Tricia Springstubb.
      p.   cm.
    Summary: Eleven-year-old Lulu explores the meaning of
love as she struggles to accept the changes in her best
friend Tilda, a teenage mother for whom Lulu babysits,
when Tilda falls deeply in love.
    ISBN 0-385-30036-0
    [1. Love—Fiction. 2. Friendship—Fiction.] I. Title.
PZ7.S76847Lu 1990
[Fic]—dc20   89-23525
                                    CIP
                                    AC

Manufactured in the United States of America
May 1990
10 9 8 7 6 5 4 3 2 1
BVG

*For Barbara, Gary,
Brendan, and Nora,
with love*

Contents

CONTENTS

1/The Emerald-Green Dress

"Jenny, human beings don't eat marigolds."

"Magolds?"

"And they don't eat mud either."

"Mud either?"

"And they *definitely* do not eat dehydrated manure! Jenny!"

"Yenny!"

"Stop being an echo!"

"Echo!"

Lulu pulled her baseball cap low on her brow. *Demented.* It was one of her vocabulary words this year, fifth grade. She'd learned to spell it, and how to use it in a sentence. "The psychiatrist said the patient was definitely demented." But nobody could ever really know what the word meant, until she baby-sat a two-year-old.

Jenny gave up trying to eat manure and came to sit next to Lulu on Grammie's back steps. She wrapped her arms around Lulu's leg and laid her head on Lulu's knee. Looking down, Lulu noticed that the top of her head looked as if it had been salted. That was from the bucket of sand she'd poured over it. Her toes were purple, from the grape juice she'd had for a snack. A button was missing from her overalls. The amount of trouble she could get into right before your eyes was astronomical. What she could do when you turned your back for half a second scrambled Lulu's brains.

And that wasn't even mentioning the tantrums.

Lulu was an only child and had no idea how uncivilized babies were. But even if she'd known, she wouldn't have refused Tilda, Jenny's mother. When Tilda asked her if she'd pick up Jenny at the day-care center on her way home from school every day, and watch the baby till six o'clock, when she got off work, Lulu said yes immediately. She didn't hesitate or worry for one instant, though she hesitated and worried about almost every other aspect of her life.

Tilda was nineteen. Lulu was eleven. The age difference didn't matter in the least, because Tilda was Lulu's best friend. Lulu wasn't like a lot of other people she knew, with a "best" friend for every month of the year. Tilda was the one true friend she'd ever had, or expected to have. Who needed anyone else? She was as glamorous as a movie star. Clever as a wizard. The most powerful baseball player Lulu had ever seen off the TV screen. Strong enough to swing a two-by-four like a chopstick.

Tilda was larger than life.

Thud thud! Thud thud!

Grammie's back door opened and the wooden steps trembled. Two turquoise high-tops the size of loaves of bread appeared on the step above Lulu and Jenny. There was a tug on the braid that hung precisely down the middle of Lulu's back.

"I'm ready."

Lulu looked up. And up, and up, and up. Sometimes when she looked at Tilda's legs, she thought of how she'd once read that a man trying to tease Abraham Lincoln about being a beanpole asked him, "How long do you reckon a man's legs are supposed to be, Mr. Lincoln?" Honest Abe replied, "Long enough to reach the ground, sir."

"Hi, Mama." Jenny had both high-tops untied in a flash.

"Now how about you tie them again, Shortcake?"

"Can't, Mama!"

"Can't is right. Trouble's your name, destruction's your game."

Lulu raised her head to smile. But what she saw froze her before the smile even got started.

Tilda was wearing a dress. Lulu had only seen her wear a dress once before. It had been pink and stiff and covered with frills, a dress as much like Tilda as cream is like motor oil.

Not this dress.

This dress was the color of emeralds, and there wasn't a ruffle or flounce in sight. It was made of smooth, soft fabric that rippled into a little green sea as Tilda crouched to retie her shoes. Jenny grabbed a fold and rubbed it against her cheek.

"You pretty Mama. Ummm."

Lulu wanted to touch it, too, but she was still frozen.

— 3 —

"Where'd you get it?" she asked, when she recovered her voice.

"At a store called the Forgotten Woman. They have clothes for real fat and real tall women."

"You mean you went shopping?"

"Where else do you think I'd get it? My fairy godmother?"

Lulu watched Tilda tie her laces in a double knot. Tilda's shoe size and Lulu's age were exactly the same: eleven and a half. Lulu tried to imagine Tilda in a store, trying things on. Countless times she'd perched on the tub in Grammie's upstairs bathroom and watched Tilda squint, pout, and stare as she put on her makeup.

But even when she'd gotten her face as gorgeous as a movie star going to the Academy Awards, she still pulled on her same old sweats and T-shirt. It was as if she only cared about how she looked from the neck up. Or maybe as if the rest of her was so long and lean and hungry-looking, with all those hollows, dips, and knobby joints, even she didn't know what to make of it. Once when Lulu and her parents were lost they stopped and asked a man where the road they were driving went. He said he didn't know. Didn't know where the road he lived on went! Sometimes Lulu wondered if that was how Tilda felt about her body.

"I mean, well, Jenny's right. It's pretty. It's not at all like your pink-and-white dress."

"That thing. My mother picked that out, not me. I stuffed it in the bag Grammie put out for the Purple Heart truck last month."

"But what are you doing in a dress? Aren't you going to the hardware store?"

Tilda started to brush the sand out of Jenny's hair. She bent close to her daughter's head, as if it was suddenly extremely important to get out every last grain.

"I *am* going to the hardware store."

"Are you going someplace afterward?"

"I'm bringing your mother the brads I'm buying at the hardware store."

"And *then* are you going someplace else?"

Tilda looked up. Her eyelids were the color of jade. She had on her fake-diamond, heart-shaped earrings, the ones that made her look like a robber queen.

"I just felt like wearing a dress," she said. Her usually pale face was pink, but that could have been from bending over Jenny. "And that's all, Paul."

"You're not . . . sick, are you? You're not going to the doctor and you don't want to worry me?"

Tilda laughed and turned pinker yet. "Sick? I never felt better in my whole life. I thought you knew that."

"But—"

Tilda stood up. "The trouble with you, Lu, is anything out of the ordinary makes your knees knock."

"Don't talk like you're my mother!"

"Then don't be such a Nervous Nelly!"

"I'm not a Nervous Nelly!"

"Okay. You're right. If there's anybody who's got the right to tell me to lay off, it's you."

"I'm not telling you to lay off. I'm just wondering why

you look so beautiful on Tuesday afternoon on the way to Ace Hardware, that's all."

"Beautiful. Sure." Tilda snorted. She jumped down the steps and swung Jenny up high. Jenny threw back her head and closed her eyes. Tilda made figure eights with her and dipped her almost to the ground. Jenny was in baby ecstasy. Flying was her favorite game, and the reason Tilda and Lulu had met.

One steamy day last summer, Lulu had been riding her bike to Little League practice. She was passing a block of old run-down apartment buildings when something made her look up. That something was Jenny, standing in a second-floor window, grinning happily.

About to jump.

And Lulu, who under normal circumstances got nervous just crossing a busy street alone, had jumped off her bike, thrown out her arms, squeezed her eyes shut—and caught the baby. Afterward no one could believe it, especially Lulu.

Lulu Leone Duckworth-Greene, who all her life had been a nothing, was a hero overnight. Until then, in fact, she had been less than a nothing—the kind of girl who trips over things that aren't there, who strikes out with the bases loaded, who'd rather die than get up on a stage. She was clumsy, small for her age, and sure her mother wondered if there'd been a mistake in the hospital nursery. Lulu's mother, Elena, was very different from her daughter. She ran her own company, dressed like a gypsy, and had more friends than she could count. It was hard to

believe she and Lulu had one gene in common—until that
fateful day.

That day Tilda had been listening to the Indians game
on the radio. When Lulu knocked on her apartment door
with Jenny in her arms, Tilda had no idea what had happened. She nearly keeled over.

"You saved her life," said Tilda. "You're a hero."

"Who, me?" yelped Lulu. "I was just riding by! It was all
an accident!"

But Tilda convinced her that she really did deserve the
credit everyone gave her. Tilda made her believe she
really, truly, was a hero.

Everyone in Lulu's family fell in love with Tilda. Grammie let her move out of the run-down apartment building
into her spare room. Lulu's father, who ran a bike shop,
baked her bread and fixed up Lulu's old trike for Jenny.
Elena gave Tilda a job in her company, which specialized
in renovating old houses. In just a few weeks no one could
remember life without her and Jenny.

But it was Lulu who loved her best. Having a friend as
amazing as Tilda made Lulu feel sort of amazing too.

Now Tilda shot Jenny up as high as her arms could
reach, which was very high. Lulu worried she'd strain the
seams of her new dress. Twenty-seven pounds of baby.
The ropy muscles stood out all along Tilda's strong arms.

"Coming in for a landing." Tilda set Jenny on her feet.
Jenny, of course, set up a howl. "I've got to go buy nails for
Aunt Ellie!" Tilda told her. Jenny put her hands on her
hips and stuck out her lower lip so far, she looked like a

bulldog puppy. "I've got to work! How am I gonna keep you in Cheerios if I don't work?"

Jenny fell to the ground in protest, but Tilda pretended not to notice. She smoothed the skirt of her emerald-green dress. It was a little short. And there was room for at least one more Tilda inside it. The high-tops looked peculiar with it, but how could Tilda wear high heels? Lulu wondered if anyone had ever tried to invent the opposite of elevator shoes.

"You be good for Lu," Tilda told Jenny. Jenny howled even louder. Grammie said she should rent herself out as a tornado warning. At the top of the steps, with her hand on the knob, Tilda turned and looked back down at Lulu.

"Did you really mean . . . do I really look . . . Shoot. Tell me the truth. Do I look like the Jolly Green Giant's wife?"

"I told you, you look beautiful," Lulu answered. "And *I* never lie to *you*." She hoped Tilda would notice the emphasis.

But all Tilda did was smile as if Lulu had put a crown on her head, and disappear through the door.

The instant she was gone Jenny stopped crying. She wiped her snotty nose on Lulu's shirt and ran off to the sandbox, singing to herself. She always did that. Grammie said part of a baby's job description was making her mother feel as guilty as possible on a regular basis.

In the deafening silence Lulu sat back down on the steps. She pulled her cap low and took a fresh stick of gum from her pocket. She chewed hard and scowled, imagining Phil "Knucksie" Niekro, her all-time favorite Cleveland Indians pitcher, watching for the catcher's signal. She shook her head slightly. Not another fastball. A change-up? All right.

Lulu closed her eyes, the better to imagine Knucksie going into his windup. But instead she saw Tilda, at the top of Grammie's back steps, gray eyes silver, the whole of her lit up and gleaming with nervous excitement. Only a demented person would look like that on the way to buy nails. Was she *really* going to the hardware store?

But she wouldn't lie to me. She's only told me that one lie, and she promised never, ever again. Why should she lie? That's not how best friends behave.

"Woowoo! Wook, Woowoo! It's rainin'!"

Lulu's eyes flew open just in time to see Jenny dump another bucket of sand over her head.

2/*Tilda Tyrannosaurus*

When Lulu first met Tilda, Tilda told her a lie. She said she was married, but her husband was away in the Navy. He wrote her ten-page love letters every night, from halfway around the world. He couldn't sleep until he did. Lulu was sure he had given Tilda the diamond earrings she always wore. It was the most romantic true-life story she had ever heard.

"Romantic!" Tilda chewed the end of a weed and spat. It was an evening last summer, a few weeks after Lulu caught Jenny. They were lying out in center field at Hart Crane Elementary School.

That night Tilda told Lulu the truth. There wasn't any husband halfway around the world. There wasn't any husband anywhere. She had bought the diamonds, which were fake, for herself.

"Oh," said Lulu.

Even though she had an endless number of questions about Jenny's father—was he handsome? did he root for the Indians? how could he leave you and Jenny? how *could* he?—she never asked one. She knew Tilda didn't want to talk about it. Lulu could understand that. There were lots of things she didn't like to talk about either. She and her mother never got angrier at each other than when Elena urged her to "open up" about her feelings, and Lulu stayed shut tighter than a Ziploc bag.

But Lulu did tell Tilda things. Their conversations always came after a practice. Lulu loved baseball. Love, in fact, was a mealy-mouthed word, compared to what she felt for the game.

"How can you spend so much time alone, watching a bunch of losers?" her mother would demand.

But of course Elena didn't understand. When Lulu watched the Indians, she wasn't alone. In a way, she wasn't even *watching* them. She was right there with them—on the mound with old Knucksie, behind the plate with Allanson, leaping against the wall, making that final out with Injun Joe Carter. Just yesterday she'd sent a letter to the manager, Doc Edwards, suggesting a new batting order. She thought Felix "the Cat" Fermin had earned a chance at the cleanup spot. Sure he was small. But he was powerful, and he had guts. Tilda agreed completely.

Baseball. Tilda loved it exactly the same way Lulu did. Every night, after Tilda got home from work, they played together. They'd walk or ride bikes to Hart Crane Field. Sometimes Jenny came, and sometimes she stayed home with Grammie.

Tilda would fire fastballs Lulu could feel on her palm the next day. She hit line drives that sent Lulu racing, leaping, and usually tripping over her own feet. Pitching or batting, she was a study in concentration. Out on the field she was a streak of light. Her earrings blazed. Her electric-blue or jade-green eyelids flashed in the twilight. Her knobby arms and legs worked like the rods of some wonderful machine. She shouted at Lulu, telling her to try harder and relax. Both at once? Lulu guessed being a natural made you a bad teacher. Still, she couldn't believe her luck that someone as good as Tilda would play with her.

Afterward they'd lie in the grass. Tilda would chew the end of a weed, and Lulu would lie very still, paralyzed with happiness and exhaustion. Sometimes they wouldn't say a word. Other times Tilda would suddenly start talking.

One night she told Lulu how hard it had been to grow up a giant.

"First I tried sleeping with a five-pound sack of rice on my head to, you know. Stunt my growth. I never ate any vegetables, and I poured my milk down the drain when my mother wasn't looking. I even tried taking *burning* hot baths, in case humans could shrink like sweaters. Nothing worked. I was fifteen years old and six feet one before I stopped growing.

"My mother hated having a giant for a daughter. One minute she'd be yelling at me to stop stooping and stand up proud. The next she'd be having a fit because I grew a whole size in two months, and how was she supposed to afford new clothes?

"And the other kids. Behind my back they called me Mighty Matilda. Tilda Tyrannosaurus. Friggin' little town I grew up in. Everybody was so bored, all they had to do was make fun of anyone different."

"It doesn't have to be a small town for that to happen," Lulu said quietly.

"Yeah. Lulu Leone Duckworth-Greene. What a name! Shoot. You might as well walk around wearing a sign that says, TAKE A FREE DIG."

"Not to mention, being small for your age isn't any better than being big. Like when you show up for second grade and the teacher tells you the kindergarten's downstairs."

"Just think, though—you'll be able to sneak into movies half-price for a long time."

"I don't like most movies. They almost all have scary

parts. Or how about when you go to sign up for Little League, and they direct you over to T-ball instead?"

"My mother never came to one Little League game. Not one. Even when I made varsity my sophomore year, plus got voted MVP, she didn't come. All she ever said was 'It's not ladylike.' This scar on my knee? Six stitches! I got it sliding for home in the district championship game. I won the friggin' game! You know what she said? 'How am I supposed to pay the emergency-room bill?' That's what she said!"

Tilda stared down at the chewed-up weed.

"Now every Sunday on the phone she says, 'Don't you know how hard it was, raising you alone, working my butt off and never having a penny extra?' " Tilda chomped hard on her weed. Fog rolled in over her gray eyes.

"I say, 'Yeah, Ma. I know. I'm doing the same thing right now.' And she says, 'Come on home. Come back down here. I'll help you out.' I say, 'Too late for that. You could've helped me when I got, you know. Pregnant. Instead you made me feel like something stuck to the bottom of your shoe. Too late, Ma.' "

Tilda didn't say anything for a long time. Lulu felt her own happiness fade along with the day's last light. She couldn't stand hearing how cruel those people back home had been to Tilda. How they'd misjudged her! How dumb they must have been! She wanted to tell Tilda that was all over now, and she was with real friends. But she could tell that for Tilda, it wasn't all over. The memories still hurt her.

Lulu searched for something comforting to say.

"But—but being a natural makes up for everything, doesn't it?" she said. "I mean, the way you played ball tonight—you're so good, so *perfect*! I mean, if I could be that good at just one thing it'd make up for a whole lot. I wouldn't care about other people."

Very slowly, Tilda turned to stare at her. She looked as if she'd just woken up and discovered she'd been talking in her sleep. Embarrassed.

And mad.

"You're only eleven years old," she said somberly.

"Eleven and a half!" Lulu cried automatically. But she knew Tilda didn't hear. Tilda went back to staring down at the repulsive, chewed-up weed.

Lulu felt as small and plain, with her neat brown braid down the center of her back, her voice that turned into a croak when she had to talk to a new person, her secret collection of baseball cards, and her chest that was still so stubbornly flat, as she'd ever felt in her life.

To keep herself from crying, which she hated almost as much as throwing up, she said, "What difference does age make? It's against the law to discriminate based on age, you know."

"Don't get fried. I'm not trying to insult you. I know you're a very unusual eleven-and-a-half-year-old. But at your age there are some things you haven't, you know. Experienced."

Lulu waited a long time for Tilda to say what those things were. But Tilda just kept on staring at the disgusting weed.

Finally Lulu burst out, "Like what? Love?"

— 14 —

"Love!" Tilda flung the weed down in the dirt. "Ha! Love! Love? You want love? You watch Doug 'Special-Delivery' Jones pull the Tribe out of the hole in the bottom of the ninth. You watch Fermin go faster than the speed of light to make that double play. That's love!"

Tilda pulled Lulu to her feet. That night they had the practice of Lulu's life. She knew she had never played better. Tilda threw her hardest and fastest, and Lulu was there. Again and again they connected. Never mind that Lulu's hand stung for days afterward. She was as bold and vivid as Tilda. She slammed the ball into dead center, then streaked around the bases. She was lightning. She was fire. She was in love.

It was that night she began to think of Tilda as her SINH —Sister I Never Had.

Then Tilda bought the green dress, and everything changed.

3/The Mystery Deepens

Tilda, who was never late, wasn't back by suppertime. Lulu told herself she was such a hard worker, this once she might have lost track of time.

"Call her," said Grammie. "Tell her I'm feeding the baby and tell your mother you're staying too."

Lulu dialed the number of the house where her mother and Tilda were working. She let it ring seventeen times.

"No answer," she told Grammie.

"Maybe they're working outside. Come eat before it's cold."

Lulu knew they were working on the kitchen today. The kitchen, right where the phone was. She sat down at the table. Grammie had made her favorite, sloppy joes, with no onions, on the kind of soft white buns her mother never bought because they lacked fiber. She watched Jenny surreptitiously take a pea and mash it into her belly button.

"You look a little down around the mouth, grandchild," said Grammie. "Did you have a bad day at school?"

"Every day's the same at school. Not good, not bad."

Lulu watched Jenny put a pea in her ear and smile, displaying a mouthful of soggy bun.

"You're demented," said Lulu.

"No, you," said Jenny.

"Then what's wrong?" asked Grammie.

"Nothing's wrong, Gram," said Lulu.

"Good."

Grammie would let it go at that. She respected a person's right to private feelings. That was one reason it was so restful to be around her. Lulu's own mother would use wild dogs, if necessary, to drag your thoughts out of you.

"I think I'll call my house and see if they're there."

Elena, Lulu's mother, answered on the first ring.

"Hejo!"

"Mom?"

There was a gulping sound. "I'm cooking. Geesh, that scallion was hot! Where are you, Butter Bean? And what happened to Tilda?"

"You mean she's not there with you?"

"I haven't seen her in hours *(munch munch).* She was going to stop and check on Jenny, then get me some brads. She never—geesh! Call out the hook and ladder! Smoke's coming out of my ears!"

"She never came back?"

"Nope. Are you still at Gram's?"

"I'm having supper."

"Butter Bean! I'm making hot-and-sour soup! And now your appetite will be spoiled!"

At least one thing was going Lulu's way today: she'd escape her mother's cooking. Elena didn't consider anything worth eating unless it burned a hole in your tongue, cracked your tooth, or made you burp for three days. She was into exotic health foods, where Lulu's idea of a perfect meal was peanut butter (creamy) and jelly (grape) on white bread, with chocolate milk and potato chips.

"My appetite's spoiled, all right," she told her mother, as the disasters began to roll before her eyes like film clips. Tilda squashed by a moving van as she crossed the street. Getting a concussion from a carton of brads tumbling off the hardware shelf. Tilda in her shimmering green dress, disappearing around a corner.

What corner? Disappearing where? Stop being such a *Nervous Nelly!*

Jenny had a pea half an inch from her left nostril. Elena was describing how much Lulu was going to love hot-and-sour soup, not to mention the crab Rangoon. And then, miraculously, the back door opened and Tilda stepped into the kitchen.

"Mama! Mama Mama Mama!"

"Tilda! You're back! I've got to hang up, Mom."

Stooping so she didn't hit the wagon-wheel lamp that hung over the table, Tilda fell into a chair. Her legs flopped out in front of her, and she hung her head to one side, like a little child so tired or sick she can't hold it up. Her arms dangled at her side, her hands nearly touching the floor. In one she held a small brown paper bag.

"Mama!" Jenny hurtled into her lap. "You home, Mama!"

"I'm home. Shoot, am I bushed." She dragged off one earring. "Even my ears are tired."

"Ellie worked you too hard," said Grammie, dishing up a plate of sloppy joes. "I'll have to talk to that daughter of mine. What a picture you make in that dress!"

A funny look came over Tilda's face when Grammie mentioned Elena. Her gaze traveled down her arm, and when it got to the hand holding the bag she gave a jump, as if she'd just noticed she was holding a lighted firecracker. Jenny, plastered against her mother, looked too.

"Present, Mama?"

"No! I mean, umm, you know. . . ."

"Open! Open up!"

"It's not for you, Shortcake! It's—"

Jenny jumped off her lap, grabbed the bag, and tore it

open. One look and she threw the bag down in disgust. Dozens of slender, shiny brads spilled out onto the linoleum.

She hadn't brought them to Elena. She *had* gone somewhere else in her new dress, shiny and slender as a new nail herself. Tilda stared blankly down at the nails, then very slowly slid out of her chair and began to pick them up one by one. She laid each one back in the bag tenderly, as if it were made of the most fragile crystal.

Demented.

Tilda placed the bag in the exact center of the table. She sat back down and rubbed her eyes, something she never did for fear of spoiling her makeup. Looking down at the plate of sloppy joes, she said wonderingly, "I'm so hungry I could eat boiled owl."

"You're always hungry," said Grammie happily. "You're the hungriest child I ever met in my life. But where does it all go, that's what I want to know."

Tilda cleaned her plate and got up for more. Twice. When she finally stopped eating it was because she was exhausted, not full. She washed her plate, dried it, put it away, and fell back into her chair. An enormous yawn shook her. Her jade-green eyelids drooped.

"Sleepy-bye, Mama," said Jenny.

"Sleepy-bye is right," said Grammie. "No playing catch for you tonight, Matilda. Straight to bed. And I'll have a talk with my daughter about working you so hard."

"Working so hard!" cried Lulu. "But she didn't even bring Mom the brads! She—"

"Shhh!" said Grammie. "Will you look at that?"

Tilda had fallen asleep before their very eyes. Jenny slid down her pretzel-stick legs and Tilda didn't even stir.

"Poor thing," said Grammie. "I hope she's not coming down with something."

"You mean like a disease?"

Grammie gave a tug on Lulu's cap. "I should know better than to say that in front of you. The World's Champion Worrier! Tilda's got the constitution of an ox, so don't you fret. I never thought I'd see her in a dress. It needs to be taken in, or let down, or something. Grandchild, I better get you home before your mother starts accusing me of keeping you to myself again."

At home Lulu's mother tried to get her to eat some of her gruesome food. Her father offered to help her with her homework. The house was full of warmth, light, clutter, and exotic, disgusting smells, as usual. Lulu concentrated on not wrinkling her brow or biting her lip, because her mother would notice immediately and ask what was wrong.

Instead she climbed the stairs to her room slowly, feeling as anxious as if there were two outs and she had a three-and-two count on her.

4/Samuel Smith

All the next day at school Lulu worried about Tilda. Was Grammie right? Was she coming down with something? If so, what? Was it serious? Contagious?

At lunchtime Lulu called her mother at work. Elena said that Tilda had come in two hours late, but how could you get mad at someone who never before had been even a minute late? Now she was working away with her usual energy and diligence. And how did Lulu like her sesame-butter-and-sprout sandwich? And the chunk of tofu cheesecake?

Lulu went back to the cafeteria. Cordelia Hill sat down beside her.

"Your mother gave you inedibles again, didn't she?" she said sympathetically. "Here, have half my sandwich."

It was cream-cheese-and-jelly on white. There were cheese puffs, too, and chocolate milk. Last year, Lulu had sometimes gone over to Cordelia's house after school and they had pretzels and root beer while they watched TV and talked. Cordelia didn't care for baseball, but she was nice anyway. She was plump, and nearly as shy as Lulu.

Then last summer her parents had sent her to sleep-away camp. Cordelia begged Lulu to come, too, but Lulu would just as soon have dived into a tank of piranhas. She didn't like strange people, places, or food, she explained to Cordelia, who wasn't exactly thrilled at the idea of going away for six weeks herself.

But when she came back, Cordelia was different. She had lost weight and she wasn't shy. Camp food was disgusting but the people were great, she told Lulu. She had landed the lead role in the camp play. Lulu said she hadn't even known Cordelia could act. Cordelia said she hadn't known either.

Cordelia was still nice to Lulu, but she didn't invite her home with her anymore. She had started to go around with some other girls, who wore bras and had pierced ears and wrote things like *MICHAEL J. IS A JERK* on their notebook covers. Even now, as she passed Lulu half her sandwich, she was looking across the room to where those other girls sat. One of them was waving.

"Thanks," said Lulu, laying the sandwich down.

"Aren't you hungry?"

"I'm worried."

"That's nothing new."

"About my friend Tilda."

Cordelia rolled her eyes. She had met Tilda and Jenny once. "Are you still hanging around with her?"

"I baby-sit her daughter every afternoon."

"You spend every afternoon with that little monster?"

"She's not a monster. I mean, she *is* a monster, but, well, she's also Tilda's baby."

"Don't you get bored, spending all your time with a baby? Don't you get lonesome?"

"I guess I'm used to being alone."

"It's not good for you, Lulu. You need friends your own age." Cordelia began to stuff her lunch back into the paper bag. "If you don't watch out, you could turn into a weirdo."

"Did you ever know anyone who had sleeping sickness?"

"Sleeping sickness!" Cordelia stood up. "You have to get bit by a tsetse fly, don't you? I don't think there are any tsetse flies in Cleveland."

"Are you sure?"

"Why don't you start ice skating? Jessica, Sara, and I are going to sign up for it this afternoon." All Cordelia's new friends had names like Jessica or Sara. Not a Lulu in the lot. "They said it's really fun. Plus it'd be good for you. Then when you outgrow baseball, you'll have another sport."

"Ice skating!" People broke bones ice skating. They got knocked senseless on the freezing-hard ice. Lulu had no use for a sport that required so much falling down. And *outgrow baseball*?

"What are you talking about?" she asked Cordelia.

Cordelia shrugged. "It was just a suggestion. See you around, Lu."

Lulu watched her cross the cafeteria. The girls with the pierced ears immediately made room for her at their table. Changing seats during lunch wasn't allowed, but Cordelia got away with it. Lulu had never dared. She was sure if she ever tried it, the lunch monitor would screech her whistle and everyone would turn to stare.

Not that she ever had any reason to change her seat. Nobody ever waved to her from across the room, wanting her to join them.

A weirdo?

Lulu had a hard time concentrating that afternoon, between worrying about Tilda and what Cordelia could have meant by *weirdo*. Once Mrs. Reilly even asked her, "Are we keeping you awake, Lulu?" Teachers almost never said things like that to Lulu, she was so well behaved. Her ears caught fire, the way they always did when she was embarrassed.

On the way to pick up Jenny she stopped at the library and checked out a book called *Layman's Handbook of Diseases*. She had taken it out once before, when her class was going on a field trip and she considered faking the symptoms of spotted fever to get out of it.

"I want you to ask Jenny's mother something for me," the day-care teacher told Lulu. "Ask her her formula for the perfect child."

Jenny, wearing a macaroni necklace, smiled sweetly.

"She's such a darling!" exclaimed the teacher. "So loving! So bright! She never gives us one second's trouble. Bye-bye, Jenny! See you tomorrow!"

"Bye-bye," cooed Jenny. "Bye-bye!" She blew the teacher a kiss, and the woman almost melted with pleasure.

"Bye-bye, sugar pie!"

The instant they got outside Jenny threw herself down

on the sidewalk. She wouldn't walk and she wouldn't get in the stroller and she was going to have a tantrum, now. Lulu couldn't get her up, and passersby gave her dirty looks, as if the tantrum had to be her fault.

Finally Lulu bribed her with a strawberry ice-cream cone. It kept her quiet till they got to the park, and also turned both their jackets pink and very sticky.

At the park Jenny dived head first into the sandbox and came up with dirt stuck all over. Lulu sat on a bench and held *Layman's Handbook of Diseases* over her face to block the sight.

The index didn't list either sleeping sickness or amnesia. It listed enough other things, though, to make Lulu herself begin to feel sick. As she read down the list, good health looked like a very small island stranded in an ocean of disease. Lulu remembered the worst nightmare of her childhood, which was that her mother or father had gotten cancer and died. She would have to creep into their room and touch them to know it wasn't true.

Could Tilda have acidosis? Beriberi? Cholera? Which one made you act sneaky, lose your memory, and fall asleep sitting up?

"I wouldn't read that if I were you," said a deep voice from beyond the book. "And by the way, your little sister just gave my little brother a right to the jaw."

Lulu lowered the book. A boy only slightly larger than she was stood in front of her. From the depth of his voice she'd expected someone much taller.

"What did you say?" she asked.

"A little knowledge is a dangerous thing."

He wore tortoiseshell glasses and had a round, but not fat, face. Behind the glasses his eyes were navy-blue and had lashes so long, they brushed his cheek when he blinked. Which he did, very fast, five times in a row.

"And your little sister is beating my little brother to a pulp," he added.

Lulu saw that Jenny had a small boy in a headlock and was twisting a red dump truck out of his hands.

"She's not my little sister. We're not in the least bit related. Jenny, cut that out!"

Jenny let go. Both babies staggered backward. Jenny, of course, had the truck, but the little boy didn't cry. Instead he rubbed his neck where she'd wrung it, picked up a shovel, and began to dig. He sucked his thumb at the same time. Jenny looked disappointed. Lulu knew she was thinking, *What a wimp!*

"I'm just her baby-sitter," Lulu said apologetically. "Do you want me to make her give your brother his truck?"

"No. Theodore's learned the art of compromise by now. Being the youngest of six children, he's had to." The boy blinked some more, like a light bulb in an electric storm. His long lashes were curly, like Tilda's after she'd squeezed them in her eyelash curler. Lulu thought she'd seen him here once or twice before, but he wasn't the kind of person who stood out in your memory.

"I don't call that much of a compromise. Jenny got the truck and your brother got nothing."

The boy shrugged. "Being the oldest of six children, I've learned life isn't always fair." He pointed to *Layman's Book of Diseases.* He said, "I hope I didn't insult you about your book. I saw you leafing through it with a worried look on your face."

"Oh." Lulu felt her ears begin to heat. This boy had what was probably the most serious face she'd ever encountered, outside of the mirror. "Thank you for your concern." She heard her own voice come out as formal as his. "I am worried. About a friend of mine."

"That's very admirable. Most people I meet don't care about friendship. They only care about being popular. What's wrong with your friend?"

"She's not herself. I'm afraid she has a disease. I thought maybe I could diagnose it."

He shook his head. "If I were you, I'd consult a physician. People today are bombarded with so much information, they think they're experts on everything. But really they only know a tiny bit about each thing. I myself pick a subject a week and study it thoroughly. So far I've done carnivorous plants, sharks, life in ancient Rome, and the possibility of extraterrestial life. Among other stuff. But most people today don't take the time. They're too impatient. Too superficial. Too . . . silly."

He sounded like someone on educational TV. Lulu remembered Cordelia Hill's suggestion that she take up ice skating. She pulled her Indians cap lower on her brow.

"I've noticed that too," she said. "Did anyone ever call you a weirdo?"

The boy blinked rapidly. "Not to my face," he said gravely. "But then, I don't have time to notice what people say. I come straight home from St. Joseph's, change my clothes, and take charge of Theodore. My mother works the three-to-eleven shift. I used to mind Peter, who's four, too, but now Helen, who's ten, takes care of him. Meg and Kenneth go to the afterschool program."

"Oh," said Lulu, awed by such organization. She imagined his mother in a sergeant's uniform.

"Theo, we have to go! I have some things to pick up at the store for Mama."

Theodore immediately began to gather his sand toys into a string bag. All but the red dump truck, which Jenny was still pushing with a loud *RUMMMM* noise.

"Give Theodore his truck," Lulu said. Jenny *RUMMM*-ed louder, pretending deafness. "Jennifer Hubbard! Give him his truck!"

Jenny still ignored her. Lulu began to rummage in her backpack for a stick of gum. "Just a second," she told the boy in the glasses. "I'll find something to bribe her."

"Is that really a lesson you want to teach a baby?"

Before Lulu could reply, he was in the sandbox holding the truck and patting a gaping Jenny on the head.

"Thank you, Jenny. You may be a baby but you have a sense of justice, don't you?"

He put Theodore in his stroller and hooked the sand toys over the back.

"I forgot to mention the study of jurisprudence. That was one of my favorite investigations." He blinked at her. "By the way, my name is Samuel Smith."

It was a moment Lulu always dreaded—having to introduce herself. Even the nicest, most polite people couldn't hold back a grin when they heard her name. She took a deep breath.

"My name is Lulu Leone Duckworth-Greene."

"I'm pleased to meet you," he said, with several blinks and not the slightest flicker of a smile. "And I hope your friend feels better."

He pushed the stroller through the playground gate and closed it neatly behind him.

5/*The Fangs of Jenny*

As Lulu left the park with Jenny howling for the dump truck, she decided Samuel was right. What, after all, did she know about anything? She claimed to love baseball, but had she ever really *studied* it? She had a job, taking care of Jenny, but she was awful at it. She stopped the stroller to give Jenny some gum. Jenny stopped wailing— but what lesson had she just learned? Terrible behavior brought rewards? If all kids were raised that way, it would be a nation of criminals.

And what about Tilda? Something was wrong with her, and all Lulu had done to help was get a book out of the library. A book where she couldn't pronounce every third word. Some friend she was.

Samuel was absolutely right. Up till now she had definitely taken a sloppy approach to life. Well, starting today, things were going to be different.

Instead of going to Grammie's, Lulu headed for the house where Tilda and Elena were working. It was a long walk, and she had to stop twice more to bribe Jenny to stay in the stroller. She pushed on. Samuel's deep voice echoed in her ears: "Most people I meet don't care about friendship."

Not me. I care about my SINH. My Sister I Never Had.

Turning a corner she saw her mother's van parked in a driveway. The front door of the house flew open and Tilda came shooting out. She sprinted down the front walk and nearly crashed into the stroller before she could put on the brakes.

"Lulu! Shortcake! What are you two doing here?"

"I just made an important decision. I—."

"Is something wrong?" Tilda was wearing another dress. This one was blindingly blue, the color of the sky on the clearest September day. Her eyelids were as bright as the spots on a peacock's tail, and next to the diamond hearts she wore a silver star in each ear. "Is Jenny sick?"

"No, *you're* sick."

"What?"

Now her hearing was affected too.

"I can see I'm not acting a moment too soon. Tilda, you've got to come with me. We have to get you to a doctor. A specialist, tops in her or his field. Don't argue. You . . ."

Tilda was crouched down in front of the stroller. She was giving Jenny a very critical look, as if she were the

— 32 —

judge in a beautiful-baby contest. All at once she seemed to make up her mind.

"You're covered with dirt and there's gum in your hair but you're, you know. Mine."

"Mine," Jenny repeated.

"Let's go." Tilda grabbed the stroller and took off down the sidewalk.

"Go?" Lulu raced to catch up. "Go where? Can't you hear me?" She began to yell. "I said I've made an important decision. I met this boy in the park and—"

"Boy?" Tilda screeched to a halt. So she wasn't completely deaf yet.

"His name was Samuel. We had a very interesting conversation. He said—"

"Why are you talking so loud?" Tilda tossed her head and laughed. The diamond hearts winked. The silver stars twinkled. "What does he look like?"

"He blinks a lot."

"It doesn't matter. Nothing matters when the, you know. Spark is there."

"Spark?"

Tilda was off again, Jenny bouncing and laughing on the stroller seat. Keeping up with her took all Lulu's breath. They went two or three blocks, then turned into a small business district. Tilda stopped in front of a shoe-repair shop.

"Is my hair messed up?"

"Huh?"

"I tried a new kind of mousse this morning, but it's already worn off. Shoot!"

"Tilda, where are we?"

Tilda gripped Lulu's shoulders. Her fingers were like ten vises. Her eyes were silver points of light.

"We're in love. That's where we are."

She made it sound like a foreign country. One where days were golden, nights silky, and every living creature knew bliss. Lulu couldn't breathe.

But suddenly Tilda's fingers seemed to lose their strength. They slipped from Lulu's shoulders.

"I mean, I am. I don't really know about him."

"Him who?"

Tilda turned and pointed to a hardware store two doors down.

"At first I didn't even recognize him. When your mom sent me there for putty, and I saw him, it was like, you know. If you saw Dennis Quaid standing by the kitty litter in the Stop & Shop. You'd never believe it was really *him*. But right away he said, 'Tilda Hubbard! You're looking good!' " Tilda lowered her jewel-colored eyelids at the memory.

"Dennis Quaid said that to you?"

Tilda opened her eyes. "Peter Mills. He was a class ahead of me in high school. He was the captain of the football team and everything else. He went with Sally White, who got Prom Queen. She was real pretty with long black hair—everyone called her Snow White. I think they were both voted Most Likely to Break Hearts. But I don't know. I never did get a yearbook." She looked down at Jenny, who had climbed out of the stroller and was stalking a pigeon.

— 34 —

"What's he doing here?"

"He got tired of small-town life too." Tilda began to look excited again. "We have that in common. He was real impressed when I told him I was making it here on my own. He said a lot of kids back home talk about leaving, but not many have the, you know. Guts. He said he finally got fed up being the big fish in the little pond. Fed up with that midget, Snow White, too, I guess. He wanted more of a challenge out of life."

She drew a breath.

"I don't know how long we talked yesterday. I mean, he talked mostly, and I listened. He said I was the best listener he ever met." Tilda's hollow cheeks seemed to grow rounder. "He said it was a long time since he poured his heart out to anybody. People in the city are a lot colder than back home, he said. When I told him people back home were never exactly warm to me, he said that just showed how blind and ignorant people can be."

Tilda slumped against the shop window. "He said he never thought of me as tall. Or even skinny. He said the word for me is . . . willowy."

It was a pretty word, Lulu had to admit.

"All day long I was waiting for your mother to ask me to go to the hardware store. When she finally did, it was like TNT went off inside me. But now I'm here . . ." Her voice trailed to a whisper. Her eyes drifted back to the hardware store. "I'm too scared to go in."

"Scared! You just said he was so nice. You said—"

"But yesterday could've been, you know. A fluke! What

if today he treats me just the way everybody always treated me, back home?"

"If he's dumb enough for that, what do you care about him?"

"Oh, shoot." Despair filled Tilda's eyes. "I wish you were older than eleven."

A whole beehive full of stings could not have hurt Lulu more.

"I'm eleven and a half," she said. "And if you want, I'll go in the store myself. What did my mother want?"

"Some number sixty sandpaper."

"Okay. Come on, Jenny."

"Tell him to put it on her account."

"I know."

"Wait!" Tilda grabbed at her elbow. "If you come in with me, I'll go."

Lulu tried to hide her smile. Tilda needed her, whether she knew it or not.

They pushed open the door of the hardware store. Bells jangled. The store was empty. Tilda looked as if she'd faint.

"He's not here!" she wailed.

A man came out of the back room. He was all dressed up in a suit and styled hair. He looked as if he should be selling silk ties, not sandpaper.

But when he saw Tilda he smiled and came straight toward them. Close up Lulu saw he had three little pimples on his square, chiseled jaw. He smelled like an aftershave counter in a department store.

"Yo, Tilda!" Slipping an arm around her shoulder, he

gave a little squeeze. He was about an eighth of an inch taller than she was. Suddenly his bright smile turned to a grimace, and he let out a yelp. "Yow!"

"Jenny!" Tilda grabbed the baby, who, swiftly and silently as a pit bull, had sunk her teeth into Peter Mills's knee. "What did you do? I'm sorry, Peter. Did she bite right through your pants? I'm sorry. I don't know why she does that. She—"

"She hardly ever does it," said Lulu. "It's only the very rare person that she bites."

Peter Mills turned his gaze on Lulu, and it went right through her. Lulu knew that look. It was the way a grown-up looked at you when he knew you were there but sure wished you weren't.

"Peter, this is Lulu Leone Duckworth-Greene, my boss's daughter."

"Also Jenny's baby-sitter and Tilda's best friend," Lulu added quickly.

"So this is Jenny," said Peter Mills, smiling at the baby. "Is that how you say hello, Jenny? You give love bites? She's cute, Tilda. She looks just like you."

How could he say that? Jenny was as fat and pink as Tilda was knobby and pale.

But Tilda said, "Really?" and stared at Jenny as if she'd never seen her before in her life.

A man in paint-spattered overalls came in then, and Peter swung around with his snake charmer's smile.

"Good afternoon, sir! How can I help you?"

The man wanted paint, a custom color. Peter slipped behind the counter and set the mixer going, all the while asking the man if he needed brushes, rollers, thinners, mixing trays.

"No, no," the man said firmly. "Just the paint. That's all today."

Peter smiled and kept on talking. His voice was rich, smooth, and flowing—an *oily* voice, Lulu thought. The kind of voice that talks you into things.

And sure enough, by the time the paint was mixed the man was letting Peter sell him a brush too.

No, don't do it! Lulu wanted to tell him. *You got tricked into something you don't really want!*

She glanced at Tilda. The gray eyes were quicksilver with love.

When the happy customer left, Peter turned back to them.

"Sorry for the interruption," he said cheerfully. "Are you free tonight?"

"Free? Me?"

"How'd you like to see *Bride of Jack the Ripper?*"

"You mean, you know. With you?"

His grin turned his squinty eyes to slits. "What's your address?"

"My . . . Ummm . . ."

"Eighteen sixteen Somerton Road," said Lulu.

"I'll be there at eight."

He put an arm around Tilda's shoulder and guided her to the door. The sound of the bells made her jump.

"All right!" she said, a wild look on her face. "If you say so!"

Outside, she leaned against the first telephone pole

they came to. Her face looked scared and bewildered. But then, slowly, a goofy, nearly imbecilic smile began to spread across it. If Lulu were coming down the street right now she'd have passed on by, never for a moment connecting this silly, limp creature with Tilda.

When Lulu spoke, the anger in her voice made Tilda jump again.

"I hope my mother doesn't need that sandpaper too badly!"

Tilda blinked. "Sandpaper?"

6/*The Red Car*

Tilda went straight back to Grammie's. She called Elena and said she was sorry, but something very important had come up. She had a, you know. A *date*. Then she hung up and started getting ready, even though it was only six o'clock.

Lulu could hardly believe it. "Didn't my mother get mad?"

"Mad? Shoot! All she wanted to know was if I wanted to borrow a scarf or some jewelry or something."

Grammie acted exactly the same way. When Tilda said

she was too nervous to eat, Grammie nodded and smiled. She offered to baby-sit Jenny, even though it was her bridge night. Lulu had been expecting Tilda to ask her, and planned to say she was sorry but it was such short notice she already had other plans. Of course then she'd say that since they were best friends, she'd break the plans. Tilda would have been so grateful. But now Tilda didn't even need her.

By seven-thirty Tilda was sitting on Grammie's front steps.

"I thought you were supposed to make your date come in and wait for you," said Lulu. "You're supposed to be upstairs primping while he has a nervous conversation with your father."

"What father?"

"Me, then. He could have a nervous conversation with me."

"I don't think Peter gets nervous. Besides, the two of you wouldn't have much to talk about."

"Baseball. We could always talk about that."

Tilda peered down the street. "I told you. He's a football player."

Lulu hated football. It was almost as bad as boxing. Twenty-two giants thundering around, grabbing the ball out of each other's hands, shoving each other's noses in the mud. A mean, messy game.

"He doesn't look like a football player. His nose is straight. And he's not built anything like a refrigerator."

"I wish I knew what his car looked like."

"You'll strain your eyes, squinching them up like that.

You'll ruin your eyesight. I think you should go inside and wait upstairs. That's what girls do in books and movies."

Tilda turned and dug her fake nails, which she'd polished "Frosty Peach," into Lulu's bare arm.

"This isn't a book or a movie, Lu. It's *real life. My* real life."

"You shouldn't let him know you're so thrilled and honored to go out with him."

Tilda dug the nails deeper. "I *am* thrilled and honored. And I don't play games."

Tilda never did anything halfway, and she could change her mind in the time it took a door to swing open. Of course she wouldn't just fall in love. She'd hurtle. Plunge. Her recklessness was the exact opposite of Lulu's cautiousness.

Up till now it was what Lulu had always thought she loved in her.

"You're amputating my arm with those nails," she said.

"Oh. Sorry." Tilda let go.

"Isn't there something about him that makes you suspicious?"

"What are you talking about?"

"I don't trust his smile."

"His smile! Are you crazy? That smile could stop traffic!"

"It looks like he practices it in the mirror. Plus he has squinty eyes. Like a duck."

"Here he comes!" Tilda jumped up as a red car with a dent in the side slowed in front of the house. "Tell Grammie I left. Tell her thanks for taking care of Jenny!"

Lulu watched as Tilda ran around to the passenger side

and let herself in. Peter Mills gave a beep of the horn and they pulled away—much too fast, Lulu thought, for a residential street.

Inside, Grammie already had Jenny in her pajamas and was reading her *The Poky Little Puppy.*

"Tilda left."

"She did?" Grammie was disappointed. "I wanted to meet her beau."

"You didn't miss much."

Grammie closed the book and stroked Jenny's curls. "It sure would be a nice thing for her to meet someone. Poor child, with all the trouble she's seen, she deserves it. Maybe a fellow would put the roses back in her cheeks."

"Her cheeks get rosy when we play ball together! Her face gets as red as a tomato!"

Now Grammie reached up and patted Lulu's hair. "Come on, grandchild. Jenny and I will drive you home."

In Grammie's car Lulu stared out the window. Tilda's disease had infected everyone. Grammie gave up bridge, which she looked forward to all week, and Elena let her work slip, even though they were way behind on the job, just to help Tilda. Nobody seemed upset that Tilda hadn't eaten a bite for supper. Tilda, who usually ate enough for half a baseball team (four and a half men). Tilda, who never got full! She was full now. Full of love. Full of baloney!

At home Lulu let the kitchen door slam behind her. Her mother hurried in and pounced on her.

"So? What's Tilda's boyfriend like?"

Not *How was your day, Lulu?* That took a backseat to *love.*

"He has eyes like a duck and he drives too fast."

Elena, who was also very short but had wild, curly hair that made her look much taller, got her *It's-time-for-a-cozy-mother-daughter-chat* glint in her eye.

"I see," she said. "Do you want to talk about it?"

"Talk about what?"

"About how Tilda having a boyfriend makes you feel."

Lulu heaved a sigh. If there was one thing she *didn't* want to talk about . . .

But she knew her mother wouldn't be happy until she "opened up," at least a little, so she said, "It makes me feel confused."

Elena looked hopeful. "That's an honest beginning."

"It's got to be the ending, too, because I have at least an hour's worth of homework."

Elena, who smelled like sawdust and stinging-hot chili peppers, hugged her and set a plate of blackened bricks on the table beside Lulu's backpack. "Carob brownies. Sustenance for the body, if not the soul."

Lulu sat down. The brownies smelled like burnt wood. Opening her backpack, she looked down the list of vocabulary words. They were past *demented.* Her first word tonight was *desolate.*

7/Thunder

After school the next day she picked up Jenny at the center.

"Was Mama in a good mood this morning?" she asked the baby.

"Mama singin'," replied Jenny.

"She was happy?"

"Happy," said Jenny, and twisted Lulu's nose.

Samuel and Theodore were already at the park. Samuel was pushing his little brother on a baby swing.

"Hello," he said. "I see you left your book home today."

Back and forth went Theodore, with little short swings like a pendulum on a clock. He was a very serious swinger. Lulu could see him in horn-rimmed glasses someday too.

"*My* swing! You get off!" Jenny made a lunge for it.

"Jenny!" cried Lulu, catching her. "It's not your swing! You don't own the playground!"

"My swing my swing my swing!" Jenny squeezed her eyes shut and waved her fists in the air. Lulu called it her witch-doctor imitation. From his swing Theodore watched intently.

"It's *not* your swing. Find something else to do till it's

your turn." Lulu turned to Samuel. "I took the book back
to the library. My friend wasn't sick after all. At least not
in the body."

"That's very good news." Samuel gave a few rapid-fire
blinks. "There's nothing more important than good
health."

He's right, thought Lulu. Imagine if Tilda really did
have some dreadful disease! Acidosis or beriberi, instead
of love. Imagine if she had something with no cure. The
thought was staggering. Love might have bizarre symptoms, but at least it wasn't fatal. Tilda would survive. She
might even recover! Relief began to sprinkle over Lulu
like a spring shower.

"You make a lot of sense," she told Samuel.

"Thank you. I'm only twelve, but I think I make more
sense than most grown-ups I meet."

"You're *twelve*?" Lulu hadn't meant to blurt it out like
that. But he was so short!

Samuel gave Theodore a push that made the baby
widen his eyes in alarm. "Twelve and one eighth, to be
exact," he said curtly. "My parents are both very short, so
I have no expectations of being a giant."

"I'm short for my age too. I hate it. You must hate it
even more, being a boy."

Samuel blinked double time. "I don't let superficial
things like that bother me."

If he was telling the truth, he was one of the most
unusual people she had ever met. If he was lying, she
knew how he felt.

"Once, when I was very young," Samuel went on,

"some other boys teased me about being small. They called me baby, and Small Sam, and the Eighth Dwarf. The usual things." He paused to blink. "I'd heard my mother say she'd found a fertilizer that made her roses grow like never before. So I ate some."

"Oh, no!"

"It was a very unpleasant lesson. Once after that I tried stretching myself. I won't go into the details." Another pause to blink. "When both experiments failed, I concluded a person's mind is the most important thing."

"Not their heart?"

"Wunder! I makin' wunder, Woowoo!" Jenny had climbed to the top of the playground's highest slide and began to bang her heels on the metal. "Wunder!" she yelled, as the metal clanged and the slide shook.

"She means thunder," said Lulu.

"That's very dangerous," said Samuel. "If she fell she could get a concussion."

"Slide down, Jen," said Lulu, even though she knew that would make Jenny bang louder. And it did.

"I want to get out, please," said Theodore. "Please let me out," he said in a small clear voice.

Samuel let him out of the swing. Though her ears began to heat up even before she spoke, Lulu repeated her question.

"You really think the brain's more important than the heart?"

Samuel's navy-blue eyes blinked. "Well. Which heart do you mean? The one that pumps blood? Or the one that inspires poetry?"

"Listen, Samuel! Thunder!"

Theodore had climbed up on the slide behind Jenny and began to bang his heels, too. Beaming at each other, the babies banged as hard and loud as they could. The slide was at least eight feet high. They looked very small up there.

"Theodore! Slide down at once!" commanded Samuel.

Clang clang! went Theodore's heels in their tiny, sturdy shoes. *Clang clang CLANG!* went Jenny's untied sneakers.

"I said slide down! I'll catch you! THEODORE!"

Clang clang!

Samuel ran up the steps of the slide and grabbed his baby brother. Theodore began to sob as if his heart would break. Samuel, carefully climbing down, looked astonished.

"That's not what slides are for, Theo! You could have been seriously injured!"

Theodore cried harder.

"I bite," said Jenny, pointing at Samuel from the top of the slide. She slid down.

"I think it's time for us to go," said Samuel. He put his little brother in the stroller and fastened the safety strap securely. Theodore sniffled. He put his thumb in his mouth and hooked a finger over his nose.

"He never misbehaves," said Samuel, looking at his brother with concern. "Being the youngest of six children he's learned the need for obedience."

"Don't you mean for never getting his own way?" The words were out before Lulu knew she was going to say them. Samuel looked as startled as she felt. "I mean . . ." What did she mean? She scooped up Jenny, who was headed for Samuel's shin with her mad-dog look. Samuel was looking at Lulu intently, his navy-blue eyes wide and unblinking.

"I mean," she said, "you didn't answer my question. I was talking about the Valentine kind of heart."

Samuel bent to check Theodore's safety strap once more. "I have to admit, it's a subject I have never investigated. Right now I'm concentrating on internal combustion."

"Oh. That's too bad."

"Why? In my experience people learn more when they find things out for themselves, not when someone else tells them. That's why I hate school."

"Someone as smart as you hates school?"

"I don't have much in common with my peers. I'm sure I'd study much more productively if left to my own devices."

He pushed the stroller through the playground gate and clicked it closed behind him. Theodore was still heaving, and Jenny was doing her best to jump out of Lulu's arms and sink her teeth into Samuel's leg. Lulu expected Samuel to make a speedy getaway. But to her surprise he turned.

"I suggest you do your own investigation," he said. "I might, uh, I'd be interested to read it."

His eyelids going like window shades in a high wind, he sped away.

8/The Red Notebook

Lulu bought a notebook with a red cover, which seemed the appropriate color. As soon as she got to Grammie's, she found the dictionary and looked up the word.

> **love** (luv), *n.* (AS. *lufu*), 1. a feeling of strong personal attachment induced by sympathetic understanding or by ties of kinship.

It was what she would have copied if she were doing vocabulary homework, but it didn't seem to apply to Tilda and Peter Mills. As far as Lulu could see, ever since she'd met him Tilda had no understanding of anything. She was completely cuckoo. And she and Peter weren't related. She skipped down two definitions, past God and country, and found:

> 4. tender and passionate affection for one of the opposite sex.

Sitting on Grammie's couch she copied the words, but they weren't very satisfying either. How could you feel tender and passionate at the same time? It reminded her of Tilda coaching her to both try harder and relax. Was love like being a baseball natural? Was it something you couldn't understand unless you were experiencing it?

A familiar shudder shook the floorboards. Lulu slapped her notebook closed. "Tilda!" she yelled. "You're home early!"

Thud thud thud! Without reply Tilda was taking the stairs two at a time. Grammie's little house seemed to sway on its foundations. *Plop plop plop!* Jenny was chasing her up. Lulu hid her notebook beneath a sofa cushion and followed them.

In the room Tilda shared with Jenny, the floor was covered with bags and tissue paper. Jenny was jumping on the bed. She had a bra on her head.

"Your mom let me go to the Forgotten Woman," Tilda told Lulu. "Peter's taking me out to dinner tonight."

The new dress was a red tube with fringes, so red that for a moment Lulu felt heat, as if she'd walked up to a life-size flame. There were flat red shoes with glittering bows, and at least ten packages of makeup scattered across the bed. As Lulu watched, Tilda hung a cascade of rhinestones in each ear.

"Don't just gawk! Tell me what you, you know. Think."

"You wouldn't want to chase a line drive in it."

"Duckworth-Greene! Does it look okay?"

"It doesn't just look okay—"

The rest of Lulu's sentence was going to be ". . . it looks extraordinary." But before she could get it out, Tilda sank down on the bed and put her head in her hands.

"I knew it. No matter what I do, I'm still Tilda Tyranno-saurus." Her brow puckered just the way Jenny's did before she let loose with a howl. "Mount Matilda!"

Lulu sat down beside her. She had seen Tilda cry only once before. It had been like a flood, the tears somehow bigger and wetter than an ordinary person's.

"Didn't you and Peter have a good time on your date last night?"

"Lulu, when we were waiting on line for the movie, and Peter was holding my hand, I felt like we were on top of the Empire State Building."

"You both are pretty tall."

"That's not what I mean. I mean, it was like Peter and I were all alone looking down on everything else. Everything and everybody else was miniature. Peter and I were the only things that were real. But it wasn't real at all."

"Oh, sure. I get it. That makes perfect sense."

"Lulu, did you ever meet somebody who changed your life?" Tilda snapped her fingers. "In one split second, just changed everything?"

Lulu looked down at her feet, which dangled just above the floor. Beside them Tilda's high-tops were planted firm and flat.

"Yes," said Lulu quietly. "Once."

"One minute you feel like you're a nothing. Even *less* than nothing. A negative number. And the next minute the world's full of, you know. Possibility."

Lulu didn't answer. She went on staring at their feet, thinking about how she sometimes felt when she and Tilda played ball together.

"Well," she said finally, "I don't think superficial things should make any difference."

"You're right. They shouldn't." Tilda stood up again. Frowning fiercely at herself in the mirror, she pushed and pulled her hair this way and that. "But in this rotten world they do."

"You're not a nothing, Tilda."

Tilda whirled around. "Could you do me a big favor? Could you help Gram with Jen tonight? I hate to ask her two nights in a row. I'll pay you overtime."

Lulu surveyed the stuff on the bed. "You're not going to be able to pay me at all this week."

"Could you put it on my account?"

"You can pay me another way."

"What?"

"The very next chance you get . . . practice with me."

Tilda socked Lulu in the shoulder, hard. "It'll be a cold day in you-know-where, before we quit practicing together."

Jenny draped the bra around Lulu's shoulders like a mink stole. Then she put the tip of Lulu's braid in her mouth and sucked it.

"Jenny! Yuck!" Tilda pulled it out.

"Nice hair," said Jenny. "Nice Woowoo." She rested her cheek on Lulu's back.

"You *do* have nice hair," said Tilda. "Why don't you ever wear it loose? Shoot, Lu. You've got enough hair for three heads. It's so thick, it makes mine look like day-old spaghetti."

"It gets in my face. I could never play with it loose."

But secretly Lulu squirmed with pleasure. She'd suspected she had pretty hair. Her mother always said so. But she'd never truly believed it till now, when Tilda told her. Maybe Tilda would suggest another way to wear it.

But Tilda had already forgotten about Lulu's hair. Looking like a contestant in the Most Savage Scowl contest, she stared in the mirror and brushed her own hair furiously.

That night Lulu watched from the bedroom window as Tilda scuttled (even *she* couldn't run in that dress) out to meet Peter Mills. The red of her dress exactly matched his car. According to Lulu's watch he was twelve minutes late, but she would've bet Grammie's teeth he didn't apologize.

Notebook in her lap, Lulu sat back down on Tilda's bed. It was covered with snipped-off and peeled-off price tags. Peter better be taking her someplace fancy. Someplace with slices of lemon in the water glasses, and butter shaped like seashells and flowers, and waiters racing over to light women's cigarettes for them.

"I wonder if Peter Mills smokes," she said out loud. "That'd be just like him."

"Like him," came a voice from beneath the bed.

"Jenny, what are you doing under there?"

"Bunnies under here."

"That's dust. You're demented."

"No, you are."

Lulu opened her notebook, and there was the first definition she'd copied: *A strong personal attachment induced by sympathetic understanding.*

So she feels like she's on top of the Empire State Build-

ing. Where she never has been, in her whole life. Lulu thought of how she felt when she and Tilda stopped at Baskin-Robbins on the way home from one of their practices. Lulu always got vanilla, and Tilda always got the Flavor of the Month, even if it was something as weird as Indian Pudding. Very often people outright stared at them: Tilda with her makeup smudged to smithereens and Lulu with sweat dripping off her nose, both of them with faces as red as fire engines. Any other time, if someone stared at her, Lulu tugged her baseball cap down or the neck of her T-shirt up. But not when she was with Tilda. Then she felt as if people *ought* to stare at them. They were so special. So perfect.

And Tilda just eats her double scoop, licking and spinning it, not a single drip, all the time lecturing me on how I have to tighten up, follow through, feel it in the shoulders. Back to basics, she says: fielding, base running, and you can never get enough BP (batting practice). Then she gets another cone, ignoring the stares, still talking, talking and licking as fast as light.

Lulu tried to imagine Tilda in the restaurant with Peter Mills. She wouldn't be eating fast. She probably wouldn't be eating at all, just melting there in her chair while Peter Mills talked on in his oily, know-it-all voice. Tilda wouldn't eat a bite, and it wouldn't be till she got home here, and checked on Jenny, that she'd realize she was famished. She'd fry a huge mess of onions and eggs, dump on the ketchup, and eat it straight from the pan. As soon as she crawled into bed, she'd start in again. Lying awake, she'd wonder, *Does he like me? Or am I a nothing?*

Lulu took up her pencil. She wrote:

> Love is when you think you're a nothing if the other
> person doesn't like you. Even if you are as far from a
> nothing as a person can get. When you are in love, the
> other person is your RFL. (Reason for Living).

She read it over and thought of Samuel Smith. What
would he make of her investigation so far? Would any of it
make sense to someone whose mind was as orderly as a file
cabinet?

9/*The Black Notebook*

After she'd helped put Jenny to bed, Lulu went home. She
studied for her vocabulary test the next day, and went to
bed on time. She had trouble getting to sleep, though, and
so it took a while to wake up when pebbles started hitting
her window at six twenty-four the next morning.

Outside it was chilly and dark. Tilda stood in the driveway wearing an Indians sweatshirt that said WAHOO
across the front.

"What took you so long?" she demanded when Lulu

came out. "You're usually such a light sleeper. And I thought you got up early on Fridays to study vocabulary."

"I couldn't sleep. I dreamed I was running down a long dark road with ditches on the sides, and *desperate, desolate,* and *demented* were chasing me." She rubbed her eyes. "You know I need eight hours sleep."

"I didn't go to bed at all. It didn't seem worth it at four A.M."

"You stayed at the restaurant till four A.M.?"

Tilda's laugh made Lulu wish words were chalk and she could erase hers with one swipe. "No, we didn't stay at the restaurant."

You eleven-year-old, innocent little know-nothing, that tone said. Well, if Tilda thought she was going to ask where else they'd gone, she could think again. Turning on her heel, Lulu said, "I'm glad you had such a fabulous time. But now *I* have to get ready for school."

"Lulu." Tilda's fingers caught her elbow. They were icy. Her voice went small and hard, as if it were making a fist. "Something bad happened."

Lulu spun around. "What? Are you okay? I knew he drove too fast! Did—"

"It's my mother."

"Your mother?" Lulu was bewildered. "What's the matter?"

"She's sick. When I got home this morning there was a note from Grammie saying that my aunt called. I knew it was disaster. Aunt Enid hasn't said one word to me since, you know. I got pregnant. I just talked to her."

"This early?"

"They live on a farm. This is the middle of the morning for them. She said my mother's had a cold for a while and now the doctor thinks she might have pneumonia. She's going for tests today. Aunt Enid says she's real weak and can't take care of herself." The fist in her voice grew tighter. "I said, 'Why didn't she call me herself?' and Aunt Enid said . . ."

Tilda swallowed, her knobby Adam's apple wobbling in her throat.

"She said, 'I suppose because she doesn't think you'd give a hoot, Matilda Hubbard!' "

Tilda grabbed an invisible telephone receiver and held it to her mouth.

"I said, 'You old witch! What do you mean I don't care about my own mother! I'll be there on the first bus!' And I slammed the phone down in her hairy old ear." *Kapow!* She banged down the invisible receiver.

"Good for you!"

"Except now I have to go. Lulu, you know how I told you what my mother's like when she's healthy? Nagging and complaining and chewing me out from morning to night? That's nothing compared to when she's sick. When she's sick every breath's her last and I'm the cause of it all. If she gets an ingrown toenail, she can make me feel like it's my fault. She's a genius, in her way. I'm going to be walking straight into living you-know-where."

"But she needs you! You're her only child! Besides, you promised."

"I knew you'd say that. That's why I came over here, so you'd convince me."

Tilda crossed her arms on her chest. It looked to Lulu as if she were trying to keep herself from flying apart.

"But today's a workday!" she said. "And I've already taken time off this week. How much can I expect your mother to, you know. Tolerate?"

"This is an emergency, Tilda. She'll understand. Besides, it's Friday. You only need to take off one day and you can stay for three days."

"But—but what about Jenny? She hates it at my mother's. She'll whine the whole time. I'll be more hindrance than help."

"She can stay here. Between me, Grammie, and Mom, we can take care of her."

"But—but I don't have the money for the bus. I better call Aunt Enid back."

"I've got a hundred dollars and seventy-eight cents in my account. I'll loan it to you, Tilda. Don't worry. Calm down. Take it easy."

"But—but what about Peter?"

The way the words flew out, Lulu knew it was Peter Tilda had been thinking about all along.

"How can I leave him? Three days! That's . . . how many hours is it?"

"Seventy-two."

"Seventy-two hours!" Tilda's inch-long, frosty-peach fake nails clawed the air. She looked wilder than Lulu had ever seen her. "Leaving him for half a day is torture! I think about him the whole time! I wonder what he's doing, what he's thinking, if he's going to call, I can't sleep . . ."

"It sounds like a rest from him is just what you need. You're exhausting yourself."

"Oh, shoot!" Tilda slapped a hand to either side of her head. "If I have to leave him that long, I'll go . . . I'll go . . ."

"Demented?"

"I can't go!"

"But you have to."

"I can only go if you promise me something." Tilda's eyes blazed. The day's first light licked her earrings like flame. "You've got to spy on him for me."

Lulu took a step back. "Spy? Me? But, Tilda, spying's not nice! It's even against the law, isn't it? Invasion of privacy? Why do you want me to do that?"

"Why do you think? So I know what he's doing while I'm gone!"

"Can't you just ask him?"

Tilda heaved a mountainous sigh. "Sure I can. But your on-the-spot-account might be more, you know."

"What?"

"Trustworthy."

"I can't do it. I'll get caught. Anytime I ever tried to do anything sneaky, I got caught."

"*You* never tried to do anything sneaky in your life. Besides, it's not sneaky. It's just, you know. Putting my mind at ease. Lulu, I really need you to do this for me. There's nobody else I can ask."

"But—"

"There's nobody else I can trust. If you do it, I'll be grateful for the rest of my life."

Tilda never lied.

"Well . . ." said Lulu.

"I'll even teach you how to throw a knuckleball. With every variation I know."

"You don't have to do that. I can see how important this is to you. I'll do it for nothing."

"Lulu, you're one of a kind. I'm gonna go in and call Peter right now!"

At school that morning Lulu bought a new notebook. This one had a black cover. On the first page, in her tiniest handwriting, she printed

The Comings and Goings of P.M.

"Who's P.M.?" Cordelia Hill asked over her shoulder.

Lulu jumped. She snapped the notebook closed. "Ummm . . . uh . . ."

"Want some Skittles?" Cordelia reached into her jumper pocket.

Lulu shook her head. "We're not allowed to eat in class!"

Cordelia popped a mouthful. The teacher never looked up from her desk. "You should've come ice skating the other day. Half our class was there. Why don't you come today?"

"I have to baby-sit."

"You could bring the little monster and just watch. At least you could see if you want to try it."

"I've got stuff to do. But thanks anyway."

"Clear your desks for the vocabulary quiz," said Mrs. Reilly.

Usually tests made Lulu so nervous, she could barely write. Once she had actually snapped a pencil in half, she held it so tight. On tests her handwriting looked like a first grader's, jagged and jerky and all different sizes.

But today, as Mrs. Reilly read out, "Number one: *demented*," Lulu wrote the word almost without knowing it. A spy! Her! How had she ever let Tilda talk her into such a mess? This very minute Tilda, clutching the $87.10 ticket she'd bought with Lulu's hard-earned savings, was speeding toward her home, leaving Lulu behind in charge of Jenny, alias Attila the Hun, and Peter, aka Duck Eyes. A spy! One of the most dangerous occupations imaginable! What would Duck Eyes do if he caught her?

"Number two: *desolate*," said Mrs. Reilly.

And worst of all was the fact that Peter Mills probably *would* do something rotten. He was as trustworthy as a baby in a chocolate factory. He had as much loyalty as a cobra. He'd probably start flirting with the first girl who walked into the store—and Lulu would have to get the details and report them to Tilda! *She'd* have to collect the damaging, disgusting evidence that showed Peter Mills for what he really was.

"Number three," said Mrs. Reilly.

But Lulu didn't hear what she said next. A window had suddenly popped open in her mind. She'd have to be the on-the-spot reporter. She'd have to tell Tilda, "He's not worth your little finger. I have the facts to prove it."

And what was so bad about that?

Leaning over her test paper, Lulu began to smile. She'd spy on him, all right. She'd *nail* him. She'd reveal his

— 63 —

snake-in-the-grass character once and for all. Tilda would never have anything to do with someone who betrayed her. She was much too proud. Much too queenly. Immediately she'd see the error of her ways. Lulu might have to restrain her from homicide. But once she calmed down, Tilda would realize Peter Mills wasn't even worth one tear. He wasn't worth anything, especially not compared to Lulu, the only person she could really trust, the Sister She Never Had.

Lulu would risk anything, for that.

10/Theodore Tries to Fly

When Lulu picked Jenny up at the day-care center, the first thing the baby said was, "We goin' the park, Woowoo."

"No. We goin' espionage."

"No espunarge! We goin' park! Make wunder!"

"We can't today. Tomorrow, maybe. Today—"

"Waaaaaaaaa!"

So much for sneaking up on anyone. Jenny was a twenty-seven-pound alarm system.

"All right, all right, wait a minute! Jenny, stop screaming for two seconds and listen! First we'll go to the park and make wonder—I mean thunder—for a little while. Then we'll do what I want for a little while. Is it a deal?"

"A deal." Jenny rubbed her nose, then tidily wiped her hand on Lulu's sweater.

Samuel and Theodore were at the park again. As soon as she saw them Lulu felt a little better. They looked so peaceful and sane, Theodore diligently digging and Samuel calmly reading. It was funny how they came every single day now.

"Tee-door!" Jenny crowed, and leapt into the sandbox beside him. Samuel looked up from his book.

"Hello," he said, with a barrage of blinks. "You're a little late today."

"We are?" Lulu looked at her watch and saw it was true. "I stayed after school for a little while and helped the librarian—"

"You don't need to explain," said Samuel, looking suddenly stern. "It's not as if we had an appointment, or as if I were waiting for you. I'm just sitting here reading."

Lulu looked at his book. The title was *Baby and Child Care, Completely Revised and Updated for Today's Parents,* by Dr. Benjamin Spock.

"I thought you were studying internal combustion," she said.

"I was. But—no, no, Theodore!"

Jenny had thrown two handfuls of sand straight up in the air as if she were celebrating New Year's Eve. Theodore, his eyes shining, had been just about to do the same thing when his big brother's deep voice rang out.

"That's very dangerous, Theodore! It could cause eye injury! Besides, I just washed your hair!"

Theodore froze. He looked at Samuel. Then he looked at the sand. Then he looked at Jenny, who yelled, "Makin' rain, Tee-door!"

"Yahoo!" said Theodore, and threw the sand sky high.

"Theodore!" Samuel jumped up, dropping his book. "What's gotten into you?" He started toward the sandbox, but Jenny and Theodore made a break for it, racing toward the slides.

"That's why I've changed my field of investigation," said Samuel, adjusting his glasses. "Theodore's behavior has become horrific, and I'm trying to understand the scientific and developmental reasons for it." He picked up the book. "I was just reading—where was it? Here. A whole section called 'contrariness.' It says—"

"WUNDER!"

Deafening metal clangs drowned Samuel out. They were up on the slide again. All at once Theodore stood up and began to jump up and down. He was eight feet in the air. Even Jenny stopped to stare.

Samuel and Lulu rushed toward the slide. When Theodore saw them coming, he yelled, "No, Samuel!"

"Yes, Theodore! You must come down! You cannot—"

Theodore took a flying leap over the side.

Lulu froze. Not again! First Jenny, now—

Throwing out her arms, she sprinted toward the slide. Theodore was a tumbling blur. Lulu's feet tangled. She shut her eyes . . .

WHOMP! Theodore hit her hard, right on the collarbone. Lulu's arms folded him in an X, and the two of them hit the wood chips.

He was safe. Though Lulu didn't open her eyes, she could feel his hot, sweet baby breath in her ear. Then she heard a little gulp, and very, very quietly, Theodore began to cry.

I did it. Again.

"Oh. Oh, no. Oh no oh no oh no."

Lulu opened her eyes. Samuel crouched in front of them, softly groaning. His face wore the same look of stupefied terror Tilda's had, when Lulu had caught Jenny. Samuel's navy-blue eyes looked as if they'd never blink again.

"We're okay," she told him gently. "We're both okay, Samuel."

"Are you sure?" His arm went around her shoulder. Suddenly Lulu smelled Dreft, the baby soap Tilda used on Jenny's clothes.

"I'm sure," she said. "Are you okay?"

"Samuel!" Theodore reached for his brother. Samuel took him, then helped Lulu to her feet. Jenny slid down the slide and ran over to them.

"You go flyin', Tee-door!" she said admiringly.

"I have to look this up in Dr. Spock," said Samuel in a shaky voice. "I don't know how to explain this behavior. No one else in our family exhibits defiance. Thank you very much, Lulu. You may have saved his life."

"Do it again," Jenny urged Theodore. "Fly again!"

"Okay." Theodore stopped crying and tried to wriggle out of Samuel's arms.

"You can't do it again!" Samuel looked down at Jenny. "Are you crazy?"

"No, you are," said Jenny.

"I better get Theodore home," said Samuel, but he didn't move. Lulu saw how white he was.

"It's okay," she said once more. "The danger's over now."

"Danger, that's the word. Did you ever notice that life is very dangerous? You never know what's going to happen. Taking a baby to a playground can turn into a disaster." He shook his head. His face didn't have a drop of color. "Danger lurks everywhere. Did you ever notice?"

"I've noticed that ever since the first day of kindergarten, when all I did was say my name and everybody started laughing."

Samuel nodded slowly. "That's the main reason for my investigations. It's my hope that knowledge protects. If you can understand something, you can control it."

"I'm not sure anything can control a two-year-old," said Lulu.

And then she told him about the time she'd caught Jenny.

Samuel looked at her intently. He began to blink furiously. For some reason that made Lulu's ears start to burn.

Jenny kicked Samuel in the shin.

"*My* Woowoo," she cried. "*My* Woowoo!"

Samuel shook his head again. "Dr. Spock warns that two is a very tumultuous age." He picked up his book, which lay on the ground where he'd dropped it again. "I'd better get back to my research."

"And we have to go, Jenny. Remember, you made a deal."

"No!"

Lulu knelt down beside her. "Remember? First the park. Then the espionage."

"Espionage?" Samuel said. He did not blink. "Espionage?"

Lulu paused. He wouldn't blab about it to anyone. He wouldn't make fun. And besides, she really wanted to tell him.

"Remember my best friend, the one I thought was sick? Well, she is. Lovesick. And now she has to go away for three days, so she asked me to spy on her boyfriend for her. When I tried to tell her I didn't trust him, and he had eyes like a duck, she wouldn't listen. But this just goes to prove she doesn't trust him either. I should have said no."

"Why didn't you?"

"Because. She asked me. And she's my best friend."

"Would you do anything she asked? Commit murder? Rob a bank?"

"She wouldn't ask me to do anything that bad." *At least I don't think she would.* "But this was something really important to her. Extremely important. I know it sounds weird, but . . . well, even though I didn't want to do it, I said yes because it made me feel so good that she asked me."

Samuel was looking at her with dark, unblinking eyes.

"Besides," she added, "if he's not trustworthy, I want to protect her from him."

"You're extremely loyal," said Samuel.

— 69 —

"Thank you."

"It's not a compliment. I believe in avoiding extremes whenever possible."

"So do I. Usually. But sometimes, with a best friend, you have to break the rules."

"I'm not sure that's wise."

"I didn't say it was *wise*." He was making her nervous. Those nearly black eyes were like reflectors, and they demanded the truth. Which she suddenly wasn't a hundred percent sure she was telling. "Come on, Jenny. We have to go."

"No no no no no!"

"Yes."

"Tee-door come, too, okay?"

"Can we?" Theodore begged Samuel. "Can we go with them? Please?"

Samuel cleared his throat. "If Lulu doesn't mind," he said.

"Huh? You mean . . . you want to come?"

"One of my investigations was into secret codes. I know about ten of them. You might require my assistance." Samuel drew himself up to his full height, and Lulu smelled him again.

"How come you smell like Dreft?"

Samuel adjusted his glasses. "Theodore has very sensitive skin. Since all of our clothes are washed together, they're all washed in baby soap. A purely practical reason." He blinked, then fooled with his glasses some more. "I didn't know you could smell it," he said quietly.

— 70 —

"Actually, it's one of my favorite smells," said Lulu.

"Thank you," he said. "You have a pleasant odor your-self."

11/*Snow White II*

"Don't you think you should have worn a disguise?" Samuel asked outside the hardware store.

"I bet he won't even recognize me. He just looks straight through people who aren't good enough for him."

Samuel screwed up his mouth. "I know the type. But didn't you say you only met him once?"

"Right."

"Then how can you be so sure of his character?"

"I can just tell."

"Hmmm."

"Here's the plan. We'll go in and pretend we're looking for sandpaper. They have about a million different kinds. That should give us plenty of time to observe him." She handed Samuel the black notebook. "Do you think you can take notes without getting caught?"

"Everything I do, I do thoroughly," he said, in that voice which was so much taller than he was.

The bells over the door rang as they went in. *Look who's here!* they seemed to announce.

Peter Mills was bent over the counter, writing something. Lulu did a double take. He was wearing glasses! Big thick ones.

No one else was in the store. As Lulu and Samuel, dragging the babies by the hands, scurried by, he looked up and saluted them.

"Yo, kids!"

In the sandpaper aisle Samuel whispered, *"That's* the monster?"

Lulu was annoyed.

"Didn't you notice how he didn't even ask if we needed help?" she whispered back. "He's completely irresponsible. Plus, now I know why he squints all the time. He's too conceited to wear his glasses!"

Jenny and Theodore began running their fingers over the different grades of sandpaper. Jenny rubbed a piece on the top of her head and the two of them shouted with laughter.

"SHHHHH!"

Lulu peered around the side of the display and dictated to Samuel.

"He's still writing. No, wait! He's putting down his pen. He's going to the window. He's got his hands behind his back. He's rocking back and forth. He's looking out. Are you getting all this?"

"Yes, but I'm not sure it's very valuable information."

"If you're in love it is. If you're in love you want to know every single solitary thing the other person does." Lulu searched Peter Mills's face. From this distance you couldn't see the pimples on his chin. The glasses actually made him look handsomer. "Write: When he has spare times he wastes it. He—"

Then the doorbells rang again.

A petite, dark-haired woman came in. She had eyes like blue marbles and full, curving lips. She walked right past Peter Mills without seeing him. Lulu watched him whip off his glasses, then sing out, "Good afternoon! How can I help you?"

Her hair was as shiny as a helmet. When she turned, her eyebrows arched, she looked like a ballerina.

"Well," she said with a slow smile. "That's an interesting question."

They walked over to the miniblinds. Peter Mills bent his head, and they talked in low, murmuring voices.

Something about a small, dark-haired woman set off an alarm in Lulu. She tapped Samuel.

"Write: 'He is giving a female customer much more attention than she deserves'."

"But you were just complaining he was irresponsible! Now he's doing his job and you—"

"Snow White!" Small, with long dark hair—it was what everyone had called Peter Mills's girlfriend in high school. This customer was exactly the same type—as different from Tilda as porcelain from stainless steel.

"It's Snow White II!" hissed Lulu.

"What are you talking about?"

Their heads drew closer. Peter Mills said something and Snow White gave a low, throaty laugh.

This was it! The evidence she'd been waiting for! A few more minutes and he'd probably squeeze her shoulder, just the way he'd done to Tilda! Then she could tell Tilda, and Tilda—

"Kitty! I see kitty!" Jenny suddenly dropped the can of varnish she'd picked up. Crash! It missed Lulu's toes by half an inch. "Kitty, Tee-door!"

The two charged headlong down the aisle. The store cat, just getting up from its nap, arched its back in sudden terror. Like the cow over the moon it sprang past Peter's head and landed on the polyurethane display. Cans went rolling. Jenny and Theodore skidded into Peter's legs.

"What the—"

"Hello, darlings," said Snow White II, looking down with a dazzling smile. "Who left your cages open?"

Samuel and Lulu hurried over.

"Are you in charge of these kids?" Peter Mills demanded. "They just knocked over my display!"

"The babies didn't do it," said Snow White. "That neurotic cat did it. I'm surprised the poor babies aren't crying! Don't you have some suckers for them, Peter?"

She was already calling him by his first name! The plot was really thickening! As Peter obediently reached behind the counter, Lulu held up a hand.

"No, thank you! They're not allowed to have junk food!" It gave her the deepest pleasure to spurn him.

Of course the second she heard the word, Jenny swung into action.

"Sucker, sucker! Me and Tee-door! Sucker, sucker!"

The din quickly reached mammoth proportions. Snow White II edged toward the door, one hand over a delicate ear.

"I'm afraid I have to run," she said.

"Don't go yet!" said Peter Mills. He threw a murderous look at the babies. "One second and I'll give you my undivided attention!"

"I have appointments!" said Snow White. "Places to go! People to see!" She opened the door and the bells seemed to tinkle instead of clang. "Things to *do!*"

A deep, sweet laugh, and she was gone.

Peter Mills rushed to the doorway and stood there, squinting like crazy, until she was out of sight. He shook his head, talking to himself. Lulu grabbed Jenny and Theodore's hands. An extremely quick getaway! Now was their chance!

But then Peter Mills turned back into the store, and Lulu saw he wasn't only angry. There was something else in the droop of his mouth, the way he picked up his papers and set them back down, as if he didn't really know what he was doing. He reminded Lulu of Joe Carter, the Indians' fielder, when he went down swinging—furious, all right. But foolish and hurt too.

"What are you staring at?" Samuel whispered. "We have to get out of here!"

"Right."

Gaping down at his papers, Peter hardly seemed to notice them go. Lulu wasn't even sure he registered the kick in the shin Jenny gave him as she went by.

12/Lulu the Passionate

"What'd I tell you?" Lulu cried when they reached the corner. "He's no good! He's a two-timer! A regular Benedict Arnold! Tilda's only been gone seven hours and—"

Samuel finished his notation and closed the notebook. "All he did was wait on a customer," he said calmly.

"But you could tell! The way he looked at her! The way she laughed!" That ivory skin! Those miniature hands and feet! Ever since she'd met Tilda, Lulu had much more sympathy for the stepsisters in Cinderella. But Samuel shook his head.

"In this country you're innocent until proven guilty. I know you want to protect your friend. I know how important her happiness is to you. But you have to give Peter Mills the benefit of the doubt. He hasn't done anything wrong."

"Yet."

Samuel nodded. "I agree there are grounds for suspicion. I suggest we stake the place out tomorrow."

"We? You mean . . ."

Samuel folded the notebook across his chest. "You're going to need a good deal of help, Lulu. For one thing, you can't go back in there again. Peter Mills isn't going to forget you this time."

"You're probably right. He was pretty mad."

"You'll need an elaborate disguise. And a baby-sitter. You can't bring Jenny. She's a dead giveaway."

Jenny was teaching Theodore how to sneak up on pigeons. Lulu knew Samuel was right.

"And most important, your mission is probably impossible."

He spoke so calmly, and looked so smart, Lulu felt ice-cold fear in the pit of her stomach.

"What do you mean, impossible?"

"If Peter Mills is going to fall in love with somebody else, there's nothing you can do to stop him. As hard as it might be on your friend, I'm afraid that's the bitter truth." He adjusted his glasses. "As I said, I've never made a thorough investigation of, uh, love. But from casual observation, people fall in love with whomever they want. It's a completely unreasonable process. In fact, if you listen to most of the songs they play on WMJI, it's usually pretty painful."

Lulu could hardly believe Samuel ever listened to WMJI. He blinked at least ten times, then looked gravely at Lulu.

"Take you, for instance," he said. "You're very brave, and very passionate."

"ME?"

"The way you saved two babies and the way you'd do anything at all for your friend. Suppose, just for the sake of discussion, that someone timid and quiet fell in love with

— 77 —

you. It would be a big mistake. It would never work out. But that wouldn't stop him. Nothing could stop him."

"But I'm not brave! I can't even ice-skate! Everybody tells me I worry too much. And nobody in my whole life ever called me passionate."

"Maybe I'm wrong. I told you, my specialty is the brain, not the heart." He handed Lulu the black notebook. "The hardware store opens at eight o'clock. I suggest we meet on this corner at seven fifty-five."

The phone was ringing when Jenny and Lulu got to Grammie's. It was Tilda.

"She's not good. She's worse than I expected."

For a second Lulu was confused. Somehow she thought Tilda was talking about Snow White. But then she realized she was describing her mother.

"She's asleep now." Tilda herself sounded very tired. Lulu had never heard her sound that way before. Tilda always seemed to have her own generator, a private source of power that never ran out. "It took everything out of her, going for the tests. She's really, really weak. I can call the doctor in a while, and see if they have any results yet."

Lulu heard her swallow. She imagined Tilda's long skinny throat wobbling up and down.

"She felt so rotten, shoot. She didn't get on my case once! She just kept, you know."

"What?"

"Thanking me for coming. I said, 'Quit thanking me! I'm your daughter, for cripes sake!' "

There was a silence. Lulu tried to think of something to say. "It's good you went, Tilda."

"I know." She swallowed again. "I wish I'd known it would, you know. Mean so much to her. How's Jenny?"

"She's great. She's right here. Do you want to talk to her?"

"In a minute. How's, you know."

"Peter Mills?"

"Yeah," whispered Tilda.

"Well, I spied on him. At work. And . . ."

"And?"

Lulu couldn't tell her. Not now.

"And he was doing his job. He was giving the customer very good service. It's all written down. And I'm going back tomorrow, first thing."

"Lulu, you're so sweet. I . . ." Tilda made a little choking sound. Lulu's ears began to burn. "It's so hard here! I'm so mad at my mother! Why'd she have to go and get sick right now? Can you believe I'm thinking that? Isn't that a rotten way to think? I must be really rotten to the core. And then she's so grateful I came—I feel like yelling at her, *How come you never said you needed me, how come you just nagged me and blamed me all the time?* I get so mad at her, Lulu—but you know what's really the pits? I'm even more mad at me."

There was another silence. First Tilda had gone limp over Peter Mills, and now she didn't like herself. Tilda not like herself? How could that be? Love was a treacherous thing, if it could make someone like Tilda feel that way.

But maybe she was just overtired. Just talking out of her head, like someone with a high fever.

"I would've hopped the bus straight back, if I didn't know you were keeping an eye on him for me. It's like . . . if I think of him being nice to me, it helps me be nicer to her. Like atoms bumping into each other and causing reactions. Like I never got up to, in chemistry. I better talk to Shortcake now. My mother can't afford me running up her phone bill like this."

Jenny took the phone.

"Mama! Tee-door go flyin'! But no sucker." She paused, listening. "I good." After another pause she said, "Bye-bye." Then she dropped the receiver on Lulu's foot.

Her brow wrinkled. She began to cry. "Mama! Want Mama!"

Lulu hugged her hard.

Back home that night Lulu locked her bedroom door and took out the two notebooks. Opening the black one she read:

GSV HFHKVXG RH TRERMT Z JVNZOV NLIV ZGGVMGRLM GSZM HSV WVHVIEVH.

There was lots more. Samuel's handwriting was surprisingly bold, with the *M*'s soaring like mountain peaks and the tops of the *T*'s tilting like telescopes. She'd forgotten to ask for the key to the code, but it didn't matter. She didn't at all feel like reading over the day's events right now.

She opened the red notebook and wrote

Sometimes people fall in love with the wrong person. But they don't care. They are unreasonable, and nothing you say or do can stop them. Love often causes pain.

But love is also like chemical reactions. If someone loves you, you become a nicer person. You pass the love on.

Oh, sure! The two definitions were like $+1$ added to -1. They canceled each other out! They left you with 0.

Lying back on her bed, she wished she had someone to play catch with. A good hard game, with the ball shooting like a white star and that nice dull crack when it hit the glove. No thinking! Just you and the ball, the grass and the sky. After a game of catch the air smelled sweeter. Things had clearer outlines, like they'd just been punched out brand new, and you tingled all over.

She sat back up and wrote in the red notebook

Loving things, such as baseball, is easier and less complicated than loving people.

She lay back down. It seemed like a very, very long time since she'd played with Tilda. With her gone there was no one else. She wished Samuel played. He would make an excellent catcher. He would remember every batter's stats, and he'd analyze every situation like a professor. His signals would be so complicated, the other team would never figure them out.

But he told me he only plays chess. He smells like Dreft.

He's practically a midget. Cordelia Hill would call him a weirdo, that's for sure. But he called me brave and passionate. And he's helping me, even though he says it's Mission Impossible.

Why was someone as sensible as he was undertaking something so risky?

13/On Snow White's Trail

When Lulu got to Grammie's early the next morning, both Grammie and Jenny were still asleep. Slipping into Jenny's room, she picked the baby out of her crib, changed her from her fuzzy pink sleeper to a polo shirt and overalls, took her downstairs, and held her over her shoulder while she wrote Grammie a note—*Took Jenny for some fresh air*—went outside and buckled her in the stroller, and Jenny didn't open an eye. She smiled in her sleep as Lulu settled a blanket over her. Lulu kissed her on top of the head.

"You're a crazy baby," she whispered, "and sometimes I really appreciate it."

She got to the hardware store corner a few minutes before eight. Samuel and Theodore were already there, in the doorway of the bank. Samuel held a very large shopping bag.

"You look different," said Samuel.

"I didn't have time to braid my hair."

"Oh. I thought it was part of your disguise. I thought you were trying to look more normal." *Blink blink blink.* "That didn't come out right. I meant, without your baseball cap, and with your hair like that, you look more like other girls our age. Their hair's usually sort of rumply and flying around, not flat like yours always is."

Lulu felt her ears begin to heat up. Was he saying she looked better flat or rumply? Was he saying she was a weirdo?

"I thought you didn't care about superficial things!"

"I don't! I really don't!" He looked confused for the first time since she'd met him. Opening the shopping bag, he drew out something neatly wrapped in waxed paper. "Here. If you didn't have time to comb your hair, you didn't have time for breakfast."

Lulu unwrapped a buttered bagel, cut precisely in half. How had he known she liked plain bagels and couldn't stand cream cheese? She was just about to take a bite when Samuel grabbed her elbow and pulled her into the shadow of the bank doorway. As she bumped against him, her nostrils filled with the scent of Dreft.

"Here he comes!"

Peter Mills was swinging down the sidewalk across the street. Of course Jenny chose that moment to wake up and begin screeching.

"Want out! Want Mama! Want breakfast!"

Lulu whipped her out of the stroller and handed her half the bagel. Peter Mills disappeared into the store.

"He's eight and a half minutes early," said Samuel, consulting his watch.

"He's usually late," said Lulu. "Very suspicious."

"We can stake out the place from here," said Samuel. "Then if she comes back, one of us can disguise him or herself and follow her in, while the other one watches the babies." He held up the shopping bag. "I brought several different, complete disguises."

They sat on the bank steps and ate bagels. Slowly, the street came awake with people doing their Saturday-morning errands. It was a sunny, cool day, and a lot of people must have decided to do their fix-it chores. The hardware store door swung in and out for men in flannel shirts, women carrying paint chips, a whole family hauling a new extension ladder—but no Snow White II. Lulu began to worry she might not come back at all. What if Jenny and Theodore had scared her off for good? Shoot! That would wreck everything! After today there was only one more day to prove Peter Mills was no good.

But the morning wore on, and still Snow White didn't come. Theodore and Jenny chased pigeons. Jenny called them ducks, and Theodore gently corrected her. They examined bottle caps and gum wrappers lying on the sidewalk. Samuel read the book he'd brought along: *The Terrible Twos: How to Survive Life with Your Two-Year-Old.* Every once in a while he read a few lines out loud to Lulu.

"It says, 'Your two-year-old is constantly exploring her

world. Sometimes she will get frustrated at what she can't or isn't allowed to do. There may be a tantrum or two. Be patient. Try to see the world through her eyes. This is crucial to understanding and loving your growing child.' "

He looked up from the book. "This sounds as if I should be glad Theodore has started having tantrums. As if he's *supposed* to."

"I guess so."

"I don't think I ever had tantrums."

"Me either. Though sometimes, now, I feel like it."

Samuel didn't answer that. Lulu was quite sure *he* never felt like having tantrums. When she looked over at him, he was studying his book intently.

At lunchtime he produced neatly wrapped peanut-but-ter-and-jelly sandwiches, apples, and Thermoses of milk from the shopping bag.

"We would've starved if it wasn't for you."

"Being the oldest of six children, I've learned you can never be overly prepared."

Jenny threw her sandwich to the pigeons. Lulu scolded her. Jenny began to wail.

"Ducks hungry!"

"They're pigeons," said Theodore.

"Pigeons hungry!"

"There she is!" cried Samuel.

Snow White II, dressed in white pants and a baby-blue sweater, was sauntering down the street. Samuel grabbed the two babies and pulled them into the shadows of the bank doorway.

"She's headed for the hardware store!" reported Lulu. "She's stopping! She's going in!"

"Here!" Samuel pulled clothes out of the shopping bag. He threw a green rubber poncho over her head and tugged on a baseball cap.

"A Yankees cap! I can't wear a *Yankees* cap!"

"This is no time for team spirit! You've got to get in there right now!"

"But—but—"

"I'll take care of these two. Keep cool. Later you can tell me everything and I'll transcribe it into the code!"

Why don't *you* go in and *I'll* watch the kids? The words were on the tip of her tongue. But looking into Samuel's navy-blue eyes, she knew he didn't doubt her bravery and passion for a second. He was sure she could do it. He was even sure she *wanted* to do it!

Looking into his unblinking eyes, Lulu felt something bloom inside her.

"Okay! All right! Here I go!"

She marched across the street. At the door of the hardware store she paused to pull the Yankees cap low on her brow. Hunching her shoulders and bowing her head, she pushed open the door.

There they were. Right by the miniblinds, exactly where they'd been yesterday, as if nothing—not time, not the demented babies, not a store full of customers—could keep them apart.

Lulu skulked around the paint remover, just within earshot. A few people glanced at her curiously, dressed in a smelly rubber poncho on a gloriously blue day, but she

didn't lose heart. She thought of Tilda, and of the look in Samuel's navy-blue eyes. Her heart pounded. She cocked an ear, listening.

"I went to several other stores," Snow White was saying. "But no place else offered service like this."

"We do everything we can to please. Our customers are very, very special people." A meaningful pause. "Very special people."

"And do you customize?"

"Sherry, you can have these blinds in any size and color your heart desires."

Sherry! Of course she'd have a soft-as-a-kitten, movie-star name! Lulu peered over the top of the Strip-Ease.

"I told you, it's a huge house. I need quite a few." Sherry flashed her dazzling smile. "I wonder if you give a discount to people like me?"

Peter beamed like someone who'd just smashed a stand-up double. "I told you, anything your heart desires. Just a second and I'll get my book—"

"Could you help me a sec?"

Something familiar in the voice made Lulu go up on her toes for a better look. A woman in a red bandana and overalls the color of a CAUTION sign was tapping Peter Mills on the arm.

MY MOTHER?

Lulu dived inside her poncho like a turtle into its shell.

"I need a little advice on these drill bits," she heard Elena say.

"I'll be with you in a min—"

"Elena!"

"Sherry!"

Elena? Sherry?

"I haven't seen you in . . . how long has it been?"

"I've been so busy. Too busy."

"I know, you don't have to tell me. How's the business? Family? Little . . . I'm sorry! I forget your daughter's name."

"Lulu? She's great. You wouldn't recognize her, though, she's grown up so much." Elena gave a hearty laugh. "In *some* ways. In other ways she's still my little two-year-old inside an eleven-year-old body!"

Eleven and a half! Lulu's ears burned.

"She's in what, then? Fifth grade? Sixth? God. Those were some of the roughest years of my life. I was *so* miserable. I thought I was the ugliest thing on two feet. A total misfit!"

Oh, sure you did!

"And you, Sher? How's your work?"

"I've got an *enormous* job right now. I'd feel absolutely overwhelmed if I weren't getting such *expert* advice here." She took Peter's elbow and pulled him forward. "Peter, I want you to give my dear friend Elena the benefit of your expertise and charm."

"No, that's okay, Sherry. You were ahead of me," said Elena.

"No, no, my business is going to take ages. I can always come back another time. Peter, be good to Ellie, now. Bye-bye!"

"Bye, Sher!"

From behind the Strip-Ease Lulu saw Sherry glide toward the door. Elena held up her drill bit. But instead of helping her Peter bolted after Sherry.

"Sherry! Wait!"

Sherry turned.

"How about . . . I mean . . ." Peter ran a hand through his hair. "It seems like we're always getting interrupted and . . . well, would you like a private consultation?"

Sherry narrowed her eyes but kept on smiling. "What do you mean?"

"I mean, uh, I—I get off work at seven o'clock tonight, and—"

"I was going ice skating tonight."

"I know how to ice-skate!"

"Good for you, Peter!"

"Could I pick you up at eight?"

"Strictly business, I assume?"

"What's your address?"

He was making a date with her! This was *really* it.

"Oh, Sher!" Elena was coming back down the aisle! "I just thought of something. . . ."

Popping inside her rubber shell, Lulu charged the door. The bells jangled, she was out, she'd done it! Across the street Samuel waved at her. The danger had been monumental, greater than they'd ever expected, but she'd completed the mission. She could hardly wait to tell him all about it.

At seven-thirty that night she pulled on two sweaters and her thickest pair of corduroys. She wished she had a crash helmet, too, but that would attract too much attention. Then she found her parents, who were at the kitchen table studying catalogs. Her father's was full of bikes, and her mother's was from a renovator's supply house.

"Could one of you please tell me why you named me Lulu Leone?"

They looked up. Her father, a quiet man who liked to make people happy, smiled. Elena stared in disbelief.

"Lulu!" She smacked her forehead. "We've had this conversation how many times now? All right." She closed her catalog.

"It was the night before you were born, and you were two weeks overdue. Cautious as always, biding your time! Driving me crazy. Your father and I went to a concert."

"It was at Severance Hall," said her father.

"There was a soloist named Lulu Leone, and her playing was so inspired, I cried the whole time. I went into labor right afterward. We figured the music was so beautiful, it convinced you the world might be an okay place after all, and you decided to make your appearance. That's why."

"I know, but couldn't you have named me something, you know. More common?"

"You're lucky," said her father. "Till that night your mother had planned on either Arabella or Zelda."

"Didn't you ever think of anything prettier? Softer? Like . . . Melissa? Or Sherry?"

"Sherry!" said Elena. "That's a dumbbell name."

"Didn't you once have a friend named that?" said Lulu's father.

"I don't think . . . what am I talking about?" said Elena. "Sherry MacIntosh! I just saw her today!"

"Is she a dumbbell?"

"Sherry MacIntosh? Are you kidding? She's still in her early twenties and she's one of the hottest interior decorators in town. I've worked with her a couple of times. You met her once, a few years ago. I don't guess you remember."

"Oh," said Lulu.

"You have a weirded-out look on your face, Butter Bean," said her mother.

"It's rough sometimes. Being a two-year-old inside an eleven-year-old body."

Now Elena looked weirded out. But before she could say anything, Lulu confused her even further.

"Could one of you drive me to the ice rink?"

Elena fell back in her chair.

"Ice rink? You want to go to the *ice rink*?"

14/The Great Skating-Rink Pileup

"Lulu! You decided to try ice skating after all!"

Cordelia Hill wore a white angora sweater and a bright red ice-skating skirt. Her white skates had red pom-poms.

"I'm really glad you came! What made you change your mind?"

"Umm . . . I . . . well . . . I . . ." There were lots of kids she recognized out on the rink, but no Samuel. He'd promised he'd come, if his parents weren't going out and he didn't have to baby-sit. It was very unlike him to be late.

"Your hair looks great!"

Lulu had left it loose and brushed it hard. The braid had made it wavy, and at home, looking in the mirror, she'd wished Tilda were there to see. But now, with Samuel nowhere in sight, Lulu felt silly and embarrassed. Cordelia didn't notice.

"Saturday night's really fun," she said. "They play our kind of music, instead of that sappy organ stuff. Some couples dance." She gave an excited laugh. "Nobody ever asked me, but I keep waiting! Did you rent your skates yet?"

"I'm not going to skate."

"That's what you think!" Cordelia started to drag her toward the rental window. "What size do you wear?"

"I can't! I'll kill myself! I just came to watch!"

"You'll never learn just watching! It's time you had some fun in your life, Lulu!"

"But I—"

"Harrumph! I mean, excuse me!"

Cordelia whirled around. Samuel must have blinked two dozen times as she stared at him.

"Wow, Lulu," she said at last. "You sure are good at keeping a secret. No wonder you didn't want to come skate with *me!*" She laughed and pinched Lulu's arm. "See you on the ice!"

"I'm sorry I'm late," said Samuel. "My father got lost driving me here."

"You didn't have to baby-sit?"

He adjusted his glasses. His round cheeks turned pink. "I have a confession. I knew my parents weren't going out. They hardly ever do. They're always too tired at night. I only said they might in case I wanted an excuse not to come here." He harrumphed again. "This isn't my natural environment."

A fire blazed in the big free-standing fireplace. Boys and girls in ice skates clomped across the floor on the way to the rink. Their cheeks were red. Their eyes shone. No one seemed the least bit worried about falling down.

"Me either," said Lulu.

"Are P.M. and S.W. II here yet?"

"No."

"It feels strange to be here without the babies. Just . . . the two of us."

"I know," said Lulu. She didn't seem to be able to get out more than two words in a row. The music started up and couples who'd been lounging by the fireplace drinking cocoa grabbed hands and hurried out to the rink. Cordelia, in her fuzzy white sweater, winked as she went by.

"I wish I could skate," Lulu said suddenly.

"You mean you *can't*?"

Lulu turned to him. "You mean you *can*?"

"Of course."

"But—but you can't play ball!"

"I hate team sports. But I taught myself to skate a long time ago. Usually I go to a pond near our house. But . . . whoa! Red alert!"

Peter and Sherry had just come in. Ducking behind the fireplace, Lulu and Peter watched them sit side by side and lace their skates. Peter pulled her to her feet and she tottered, falling against him and laughing. He was more than a foot taller than she was. She wore a tiny fluffy pink sweater and tiny, very tight jeans. Thumbelina on skates. They disappeared through the door to the rink.

"Come on! Get some skates on!" cried Samuel.

"Can't we just watch them from the bleachers?"

"Then you won't know what they're saying to each other. Maybe they really did come here to discuss miniblinds. Maybe it's all totally innocent."

"Samuel! That's ridiculous!"

"We still don't have any hard evidence. They'd laugh us out of court with the circumstantial hearsay we have. Besides, you said your friend wanted to know every single solitary detail. And didn't you say you'd do anything for your friend?"

The skates felt worse than anything she'd imagined. They seemed to cut off the circulation to her feet. And maybe to her brain too. When Samuel linked arms with her, her whole mental system went haywire.

They paused at the entrance to the rink. Sherry sailed by, in the crook of Peter's arm like a little china doll. Tilda would never have fitted there so neatly.

Thinking of Tilda settled Lulu's discombobulated brain. "I'll try it," she said to Samuel.

He looked as if he'd never doubted she would. He believed she was brave and passionate. He really did.

Maybe I am.

"Let's go," she said.

She fell down immediately. Her feet flew up, her bottom crashed down. The ice was as cold and hard as she'd always imagined.

Before she could pull herself up on the side of the rink, two guards in yellow jackets flew over and got her by the armpits. Of course everybody turned to see who the uncoordinated klutz was.

"Are you all right?" they both asked at the same time.

As soon as I get off this rink I will be.

But Samuel had other ideas.

"Good. You fell down. Everybody has to fall down be-fore he or she can learn."

"I bet you never fell down!"

"Move along, please," said the guards at the same time.

"You're attracting attention," said Samuel. "You-know-who will notice." He took her arm. "Just hold on to me. You'll get the hang of it soon. You're too stiff. Bend your knees. March. Now glide."

He was a natural. She could never learn from him. He was scanning the ice, whizzing along, while it took every ounce of her concentration just to stay upright.

"Where'd they go?" he said. "They must be behind us. Keep your ears open as they go by."

". . . much stronger than you look," Peter Mills was bending to say. He didn't have his glasses on. Any second he might crash into someone else. He was endangering the entire rink, because he was conceited. A menace to humanity, that's what he was! Sherry's husky laugh flew over her shoulder as they glided by.

Lulu felt sick to her stomach. But Samuel pulled her on, around and around. Her feet were in agony. Cordelia waved merrily and rolled her eyes as she passed them. She went slowly and wobbily, but she passed them. Every-one did, even one girl who couldn't have been more than five.

". . . tired of being a big fish in a little pond," Peter said the next time by.

"He's saying the same things to her as he did to my friend," Lulu told Samuel. She started to go over backward and he grabbed her. "Peter Mills is a terrible person! A fake and a cheat!"

"Were he and your friend engaged to get married?"

"No!"

"Were they going steady? Did they have an understanding?"

"They only had two dates, Samuel!"

"Then why can't he take another girl ice skating?"

"Because! I told you! Tilda loves him! She gave him her heart!"

Lulu forgot herself. She threw out both arms. A big mistake. Her feet went in two directions. Then they went in two more directions. Her back made a perfect arch. Her hands flew up as if to ward off a grizzly bear. She saw the alarm on Samuel's face. He reached out to catch her. Another big mistake. *Crash!* First she hit the ice, and then Samuel hit her.

"WHAT IN THE . . . !"

Two more bodies hurtled through the air and landed with terrible thuds beside them. "Ugh!" yelled one of the bodies. It was a regular pileup. The guards in their yellow jackets raced over. Lulu saw Samuel's glasses lying on the ice. Not cracked, thank goodness. One of the other bodies reached out a hand to pick them up. A very small chinawhite hand with perfect oval nails. S.W. II! Holding the glasses, she was on her feet before anyone could touch her. With her empty hand she dusted off her size-one jeans.

"Are you kids all right?" she asked anxiously.

Lulu still hadn't moved. She knew you weren't sup-

posed to move a person who had shattered every bone in her body. But then she saw a look flicker across S.W. II's heart-shaped face. *Don't I know these kids from somewhere?* Lulu knew she had to act.

Scrambling up, she pretended to accidentally slip again and bump Snow White. Snow White reeled back, and the glasses flew out of her hand. This time they landed with a *crack*. Meanwhile Snow White went back against Peter Mills, who was just getting up.

"Oof!" He was down again. He threw out a hand to break his fall and a passerby almost skated over it. "Ugh!" Finally he got to his feet. It was very plain he didn't enjoy looking foolish.

Meanwhile Samuel retrieved his glasses and gave Lulu a hand up. Without a word he slipped an arm around her and hauled her off the ice.

They hid behind the lockers and spied on Peter and Sherry as they took off their skates. Peter definitely did not look happy. But Snow White was smiling! Though they couldn't hear their conversation, Lulu thought she was teasing him. She looked like someone who loved mischief. Someone who did what she wanted, no matter what, and didn't bother about feeling guilty afterward. Lulu supposed only beautiful women with husky laughs could get away with that attitude toward life.

They stood in the doorway and watched the red car pull away. For the sake of humanity Lulu hoped Peter Mills wore his glasses when he drove, at least.

"I guess we'll have to let the trail go cold," Samuel said.

Lulu had a feeling he meant "for good." At least as far as

he was concerned. She watched him rub his shin, then try to stick the temple back on his glasses.

"The hinge is broken," he said.

"I'm sorry I made you fall," she said. "Thanks for trying to catch me."

Samuel looked down at the toe of his ice skate. *Blink blink blink!* His long curly lashes brushed his cheek. "You caught Theodore, after all. I owed it to you."

Now that we're even, I don't owe you anything further. I can stop this pointless, ridiculous, dangerous *espionage and get back to my thorough investigations.* He was much too polite to say any of that, but Lulu knew it must be what he was thinking. With a heavy heart she tried to apologize.

"You're right about my friend not having any claim on Peter Mills. Plus, who'd want him? He's so conceited and he has pimples and smells like a perfume counter."

But Samuel continued to stare at his well-worn ice skate. "Love is unreasonable," he said quietly. "Your investigation has determined that beyond a doubt."

Lulu thought of Tilda, back home dreaming of Peter Mills. "Love causes pain," she said.

Samuel massaged his shin. "That's for sure."

15/Lulu Alone

Before their parents came to pick them up, Samuel transcribed the night's events into the black notebook. He was at it for a very long time. It was just like him to be so thorough, even though he was washing his hands of the case.

"I'd better teach you how to read this," he said, handing her the notebook. In a hushed voice he explained that *A* equaled the code letter *Z*, *B* equaled *Y*, and so on, except for *Q*, which equaled the code letter *U*, and *F*, which equaled the code letter *J*, just to throw in a little extra confusion.

"I've got it," said Lulu.

"When you get home, read it over and verify it," he instructed. "Please read it very thoroughly, *tonight.*"

They shook hands. Samuel had the worst blinking fit Lulu had ever seen. Or maybe it just seemed that way, without his glasses on.

As she watched him climb into an enormous, slightly dilapidated station wagon driven by a very short man, Lulu clutched the black notebook to her chest. Now she was on her own. It was amazing someone as sensible as

Samuel had helped her as long as he had. Who could blame him for deserting her now?

It wasn't enough that she'd never see Samuel again. When Lulu got home, her mother had to be on the phone. Tilda should have called much earlier. By all rights Lulu should have missed her call. But from what her mother was saying, and the way she was rummaging through her forest-fire hair and squeezing her face into its most concerned expression, Lulu knew she was talking to Tilda. And not a happy Tilda either.

"Don't worry about it! I know we're behind, but a house is just a house! It'll be there tomorrow. A mother's a different story! You stay there just as long as she needs you! I'll manage—oh, here's Lulu!"

Disappearing juice! What Lulu wouldn't have given for a bottle of it. But her mother was holding out the receiver and whispering, "She has to stay longer than she thought. Tell her it's okay! Tell her Jenny's fine and everything else too!"

Lulu took the phone. "Hi, Tilda."

"Shoot, it's good to hear your voice."

She sounded so subdued, Lulu's heart began to pound.

"Is your mother . . . ?"

"She has pneumonia. They put her in the hospital. She's not gonna, you know. You know. They don't think. But when people are old, pneumonia can be serious. It can have complications."

"That's awful, Tilda."

"Shoot. She looked so bad this morning when I went in

to her, for a second I thought she already—" Tilda broke off, and Lulu could imagine her Adam's apple wobbling up and down her thin throat. "When they said she had to go into the hospital, at first I was so relieved. I was so glad, knowing she was gonna get the right care!

"But then it hit me like a John Deere combine—the hospital! It's thirty miles away! How am I gonna get her there? And how are we gonna *pay* for it? They started shoving all these forms at me, and I knew there were important questions I should probably be asking the doctors, and all I could think was *I'm gonna mess this up! Screw things up good!* I was scared out of my gourd. I couldn't even move.

"But then my mother called me, she needed something, and I *had* to move, and shoot. I didn't stop moving till now.

"First I called my Aunt Enid, because she has a car, and she said sure, she'd drive my mother to the hospital. She was almost nice to me, Lu. She stopped herself short of being kind, but she was almost nice. Then when we got to the hospital I just took a deep breath and told myself we're taking this one step at a time here. So I read the forms as carefully as I could, and instead of pretending I knew what I was doing I asked a whole lot of questions, and if I got the answer and still didn't understand I asked again, and nobody said I was dumb, at least not to my face. So I did it. And you know what happened?"

"What?"

"Once we finally got my mother comfortable in the hospital bed, she grabbed hold of my hand. And she, you know. She wouldn't let go. I had to sit there till she fell asleep."

Lulu knew Tilda wasn't telling this story to show how selfish her mother was.

"She really appreciated you," she said.

"Yeah. I guess she did."

"She should."

"You start thinking things in a hospital. Shoot, they're bad places! Things you probably wouldn't think anyplace else. She looked so little and old lying there, she made me feel so big and strong. It might be the only time in my life, off a baseball diamond, that I ever felt, you know. Able. It was almost like *I* was the mother. And I was thinking, shoot. We never gave each other a whole lot of chance."

Tilda didn't say anything for a while. Then she went on.

"So I guess I need to stay a few more days. Your mom says not to worry. But how's Jenny doing?"

"She's fine. You know she feels real secure with us. Mom can take her to day care on Monday, and I'll pick her up, the same as usual."

"I sure miss you all."

Sudden tears pushed at the backs of Lulu's eyes. And then Tilda popped the question she'd been dreading.

"Peter?"

"He seems . . . the same."

"I was gonna call him today, at the store. Just to surprise him. But I didn't get the chance." She gave a short, sad laugh. "Shoot. I didn't even think about him all day, till now."

"That's probably for the best."

"Yeah. He probably wouldn't have had time to talk on the phone today. Saturday, he must have been really busy. You really spied on him again for me? You're something else."

"Samuel and I did."

"Who?"

"The boy I met at the playground."

"The real serious one?"

"Yeah."

Tilda's voice teased, "So you have a boyfriend too. My mother always said it was the quiet ones you had to watch."

"Samuel says love is very unreasonable."

Tilda didn't laugh. Instead she was quiet for a moment. Then she said, "You know what I was thinking about love? I was thinking it while I sat by my mother's bed tonight."

"What?"

"I was thinking it's, you know. Seeing the world through somebody else's eyes. Or trying to."

Then Tilda said she'd call earlier tomorrow, so she could talk to Jenny.

"Bye."

"Bye."

Upstairs in her room Lulu opened the red notebook. She wrote:

> Love is seeing the world through someone else's eyes. Or trying to.

She lay back on her bed. Her feet still throbbed. Her rear end was sore from the ice. Closing her eyes, she saw Samuel reaching out, trying to catch her.

She opened her eyes. *Blink blink blink!* She tried it again. *Blink blink blink!* The world leapt and flickered, like candles on a birthday cake.

16/The Most Dangerous Thing of All

The next day was Sunday. The hardware store was closed. When Lulu got to Grammie's, to baby-sit while Grammie went to church, she pulled out the phone book and looked up Mills.

"Twenty-two of them," she told Jenny, who was wrapping a scarf around and around her neck. "Three of them named Peter, and one with initial *P.* Which one's *our* Peter Mills?"

Jenny began to wrap a scarf around Lulu's neck. "Ready, Woowoo."

"Ready for what?"

"Go get Tee-door."

Lulu didn't have the heart to tell her she might never see Theodore again. Gently she said, "I don't know if Theodore will be at the park today. It's Sunday."

"Sunny day," Jenny agreed.

She was right. The sky was as clear and blue as Lulu had ever seen it. It was heartless of the sky, to be so glorious on a day when her best friend was miles away and the only other person she'd ever really talked to had washed his hands of her. Thunderclouds or cold drizzle would have been much more appropriate.

"We goin' now," the baby announced. "Time to go."

Lulu copied the addresses of the five possible Peter Millses, and slipped Grammie's city map into her backpack. *Blink blink blink!* As they walked along she made trees, houses, and passing cars leap and flicker. She remembered Samuel's glasses on the ice. His horrified look as she pulled him down on top of her. She tried to prepare herself, but still the sight of the empty playground was very depressing.

Jenny flung herself across a swing and went back and forth, trailing her fingers in the wood chips. Desolate. She was probably thinking, *First my mother deserts me, and now my buddy Tee-door. It's a rotten world, just like Mommy says!*

A spiderwebby old tennis ball lay beneath a bench, and Lulu began to bounce it against the locker where arts-and-crafts supplies were kept in summer. Toss, bounce, catch. *Thud, thwok, plop.* If it weren't for Tilda, she could be home reading old *Baseball Digests.* That's what she did, between the World Series and spring training. If it weren't for Tilda, she could be back at Grammie's, eating one of the jelly doughnuts Grammie always brought home from the bakery after church. She could be at the white metal kitchen table, listening to Grammie sing "Nearer, My God, to Thee" while she got the Sunday roast ready for the oven, watching Jenny poke her finger in a dough-nut and suck off the custard. Instead here she was at a ghost playground, wondering what to do next.

She thought of Tilda's voice on the phone last night. That deep, deep sadness as she wondered if she and her mother had squandered their chances together. *Love is seeing the world through someone else's eyes.*

Life was dangerous, just as Samuel said. Samuel knew! One minute you were skating, the next you were part of a four-body pileup. One minute you thought your mother had ruined your whole entire life, and you despised her— the next minute she was in bed, holding on to your hand for dear life, and you wondered how the two of you had messed up so bad. Very dangerous. Danger at every turn. People thought love would save them. But Samuel was right again. Love was the most dangerous thing of all.

That rotten Peter Mills! It was all his fault! Lulu threw the ball so hard, it ricocheted over her head. She chased it and scooped it up the way Tilda had shown her. That scum! That two-timer! If things were ever going to be right again, she had to get him out of the picture *once and for all*!

She sat down on a bench and pulled out the city map. Locating each of the five possibilities, she saw that one address was very near the hardware store. It had to be him. She and Samuel had seen him walking to the store.

Lulu threw the tennis ball into her backpack.

"Come on, Jen. No Tee-door today. It's just you and me."

They crossed the street to the gas station, where Lulu borrowed a phone book and called a taxi company.

"The corner of Euclid Heights and Lancashire," she said, in as deep a voice as she could muster. "On the double. Please."

She wasn't going to be left with a cold trail again. This time if old Duck Eyes decided to drive away, she'd be right behind him.

17/Follow That Car!

The cab took so long to get there, Lulu had to buy Jenny a can of ginger ale to keep her quiet. Maybe they'd decided she was just a kid playing a trick, and they weren't sending a taxi after all.

But then she saw it, coming toward them down the deserted Sunday street.

"Here it comes, Jen!" she cried, at the exact same moment the baby yelled, "Tee-door!"

Samuel and Theodore were just arriving at the playground. "Tee-door! Tee-door!" Jenny screeched, and the brothers turned to peer across the street as the taxi rattled to a stop.

"Someone here call a cab?" The driver, who had sandy hair and freckles and barely looked old enough to drive, eyed Lulu suspiciously. He was chewing a huge wad of gum.

"That's right," she said. The way he looked at her made her realize she had no idea how much a taxi cost. Probably more than two dollars, though, which was about how much she had in her backpack.

"Lulu! What are you doing?" Samuel, pushing Theodore's stroller at about ninety miles an hour, raced up to her. He wore a navy-blue suit with a white shirt and a navy-and-white polka-dot tie. His hair was combed straight back, and his navy-blue eyes looked at her without blinking. For a moment Lulu almost forgot the answer to his question, he was so startlingly handsome.

"I'm—I'm tailing you-know-who. This time I'm not letting him get away." She turned to the cabdriver. "Twenty-two forty-seven Silsby Road," she said, in the masterly voice of someone who took cabs every day. "And step on it."

"Sorry, kiddo, but you're not going around the block till I see the fare." Slouching behind the wheel, the driver blew an enormous, bored bubble.

"Will this do?" Samuel pulled a wallet from his pants and held up a ten-dollar bill.

"Hop in," said the driver.

For a moment Lulu couldn't speak. Samuel was so cool! He was like someone in a movie! He was as smooth as Peter Mills, without the conceitedness!

"Where'd you get so much money?" she asked finally.

"Obviously you didn't read over the secret code," he said. Bending to fold the stroller, he added, in an uneasy voice, "Or maybe you did."

"I guess I forgot."

"Oh." He sounded relieved. He straightened his tie and adjusted his glasses. The broken temple was stuck back on with adhesive tape. The cab took off. The backseat was like a cave and Jenny and Theodore staged a two-baby circus, rolling on the floor and jumping on the seat. Being out of car seats made them delirious. Samuel grabbed Jenny just before she kissed the back of the cabdriver's neck. All this was very dangerous, of course, but he didn't point that out. He seemed to have other things on his mind.

"I had come to the same conclusions on P.M.'s address," he said. "But I wasn't sure it was worth pursuing at this point."

"Anything worth doing is worth doing thoroughly," said Lulu.

They instructed the driver to pull over a few houses down from 2247 Silsby. It was a narrow street, crammed with two-family houses whose porches sagged and steps crumbled.

"Please keep the motor running," said Samuel.

"This is gonna cost you," said the driver, eying them in the rearview mirror. Samuel pulled out a five-dollar bill and waved it at him. He let the engine idle.

Sure enough, before ten minutes had gone by the red car backed out of the driveway of 2247. It took off up the street, exceeding the speed limit by at least ten miles an hour.

Samuel gripped the back of the cabbie's seat.

"Follow that car!" he cried. He turned to Lulu. "I can't believe I got the chance to say that in real life."

The cab jolted to life, flinging them back in their seats. *Real life.* She was in a speeding cab, on the tail of a cheat and a fraud, sitting next to a devastatingly handsome boy who could ice-skate as well as anyone and apparently was secretly wealthy. The facts of the matter flooded over her. She was doing this. She, the world's most Nervous Nelly, the weirdo of her class, the nothing. This was her *real life.*

"Yahoo!" yelled Jenny, and Samuel laughed. It was like the sound an exotic bird at the zoo might make, finding its cage door left open. Thrilling and beautiful.

18/ Case Closed

The red car drew up in front of a well-kept double on a quiet side street. Peter Mills gave his horn a jaunty little beep, but no one came out. He beeped again, but still no reply. Lulu and Samuel watched him climb out of the car and go up to the front door.

"I told Tilda she shouldn't sit on the front steps," said Lulu.

Peter Mills seemed to be inside for a very long time. The cab's meter was up to $11.65. But then the house's front door opened, and out came Peter with Snow White II, dressed in palest pink. Peter held the car door for her. He pulled away from the curb with a squeal of tires.

The cab took off after them. Lulu thought by now the driver was enjoying the chase too. He cracked his gum and ran a red light. Lulu steeled herself for the siren, the flashing blue light chasing them. But no police had seen them. They'd gotten away with it.

The red car pulled into the lot of the Mayland Cinema.

"The movies? On a day like this?"

The cabbie pulled over, just past the parking-lot entrance.

"What've you kiddos got in mind now?"

He was at their beck and call, a genuine grown-up (even if he did still chew bubble gum). Lulu wanted to tell him to wait there, and keep the engine running. That was how they'd do it on TV. But the meter was already up to $12.50.

"I guess we'll get out."

Samuel handed the driver the fifteen dollars.

"And keep the change," he said.

Lulu could tell that was something he'd always wanted to say in real life, too. Lucky for them Peter Mills was a skinflint and had taken Sherry to the dollar movie. She fished the two dollars out of her backpack. The ticket taker must have been half asleep, because even though the film was PG-13, she let them in without any questions.

Or could it be they somehow, for the first time in their lives, looked older than their ages?

The theater was almost empty. It was easy to spot Sherry and Peter sitting in the next-to-last center row. He held an enormous tub of popcorn. While he stuffed in huge handfuls, Sherry stared straight ahead, intent on the coming attractions.

"We better not sit too close," whispered Lulu. "I don't trust Jenny and Theodore."

They sat one row back, across the aisle.

"We won't be able to hear their conversation," said Samuel. "But then, most people don't come to the movies for conversation."

The movie was *Midnight on Sycamore Street, Part 7,* exactly the kind of movie Lulu would never, ever have watched, even at home with both her parents there and all the lights on. It was gruesome. It was grisly. It was ghastly. Within five minutes one person had her hand bitten off, another one got pulled into a grave, and a whole house went up in purple-green flames

"It's mean!" cried Jenny. "Don't like it! Make it go away!"

"Don't worry," Lulu whispered. "It's just pretend."

"Don't like it!" yelled Jenny.

"It can't hurt you!" whispered Lulu.

"Don't like it!" yelled Jenny.

"Me either," said Theodore.

"Sssh!" said Samuel.

But he needn't have worried about Sherry and Peter hearing them. Peter stuffed in another handful of popcorn and set the tub by his feet. Then he stretched his arm way over his head and landed it across Sherry's shoulders. Sherry stared attentively as a coffin lid slowly opened.

Samuel scribbled furiously in the dark.

Something that resembled a million worms shaped into a human body began to rise from the coffin.

"Don't like it!" yelled Jenny.

"Hide down here," said Theodore. Both babies slid down onto the floor.

Lulu felt awful. How could she have taken poor Jenny in here? This was no movie for a two-year-old! What if Jenny had nightmares? What if she became even more demented? *What if I have nightmares?* This was no movie to take *anyone* to. It figured Peter Mills would choose it! He probably thought Snow White would faint dead away in his big strong arms. Hide her china-doll face against his big strong chest!

But ha! Snow White was watching the film as if she loved every minute of it. She hadn't taken her eyes off the screen since it started.

In the dark Samuel's pen scratched across the paper at a hundred miles an hour.

Peter Mills didn't seem to notice that Sherry was more interested in ghouls than him (as if there was much difference!). He didn't have his glasses on, so he probably couldn't see anything, anyway. Lulu watched as he moved as close to Sherry as possible. He put his lips against her hair. Sherry tossed her head as if a fly had buzzed in her ear. Peter leaned across the armrest. Sherry leaned farther away. Peter leaned. Sherry leaned. Peter took her chin in his hand. He turned her face toward him. He bent his lips to hers.

"Aaaargh!" He let loose with a terrified howl and began to kick his left leg as if one of the monsters had leapt off the screen and onto his shoes. "Let me go!" He sprang up, flinging Sherry backward. "I said, let me go, you . . ."

The few other people in the audience turned to look. S.W. II gave a sudden, husky laugh.

"It's a couple of babies! That's all, Peter! Calm down."

"Babies? Again? Where are all these babies coming from?"

"Will you stop yelling? Here we've got a couple of poor lost babies and you're yelling at them!"

"That one bit me! I swear it did!"

A man with a flashlight came running down the aisle.

"I'm the manager! What's the problem here?"

"The problem is there's a couple of little demons loose in here. That's what the problem is!"

The manager shone his flashlight on the floor. "How'd you two get in here?"

"Woowoo and Samwell," said the voice. This time it was full of popcorn.

"If I need a tetanus shot I'm billing the theater," said Peter.

"Darling," said Snow White II. "Are you for real?"

"I guess I'll have to take them to my office," said the manager. He didn't exactly sound as if he was looking forward to it.

Lulu and Samuel stood up and crossed the aisle. This time, even in the dim light, without his glasses, Peter Mills recognized them.

"You two! Again!" The blood drained from his face. He looked just like the woman in the movie before she got her hand bitten off. "I can't believe it! What are you kids, some kind of secret police or something? What is this? What are you following me around for?"

"Examine your conscience," replied Samuel in his deep, deep voice.

"Pipe down back there!" someone yelled from a front row. "Quiet in the rear!"

Snow White picked up her purse from the seat and smoothed her pale pink skirt. Peter Mills said, "Wait a minute, Sher. We're not leaving till I get to the bottom of this."

"*You* may not be leaving. But I am."

Peter Mills's mouth fell open. His squinty eyes grew very round.

"What do you mean?"

"I mean, I don't know what's going on around here, but I have the sneaking suspicion you deserve it." She threw a glance at the screen, where the worm corpse was letting itself in someone's bedroom window. "Too bad. I adore horror movies."

Looking back at Peter, she smiled and chucked him under the chin. "I still need those blinds. I'll phone my order in Monday."

"But . . . wait a minute! I don't get it! What—"

"Peter, darling! You'll still get my business! Don't fret! But let me give you a little advice. Business and pleasure don't mix! No, no, no! If you're as serious about getting ahead as you say you are, remember that! Repeat it to yourself ten times a day!"

"But I don't get it! I thought we . . . you acted like . . ."

Sherry shrugged her shoulders and flashed her dazzling smile. "You had me temporarily confused. I almost broke my own rules—I admit to being human! You've got the charm, Peter, there's no doubt about that! But if you really mean to have a career, you'll also have to develop the . . ." She tapped his forehead.

"Sherry, you don't mean . . . You mean you're walking out on me?"

"I'll call you Monday with that order." She patted Jenny and Theodore on the heads. "Bye-bye, you guys. You're surreal, you know that?"

"No, you," said Jenny.

"Quiet in the rear!"

Sherry swung up the aisle.

"Sherry! You can't! Nobody ever . . ."

She was gone.

Peter stood in the aisle, arms hanging at his sides, staring at the exit. He looked like a rookie whose manager had just sent him back to the minors. Forever.

"You can't . . ." he repeated.

"She can," said Samuel.

"She can!" Jenny repeated gleefully.

"Tell us the truth, Peter," said Lulu. "What was really going on? Were you selling her miniblinds? Or . . . you know."

Peter fumbled in his shirt pocket. He pulled out his glasses and put them on. They really did make him look more handsome. Lulu almost told him. But he probably wouldn't have heard. He kept staring at the exit.

"When she told me about the mansion she was doing over, I figured it was my big chance." His voice was hollow, like an echo of an echo. Behind him, on the screen, horrible things were happening. "I figured if I could get her to buy all the paint and hardware and window treatments from us, maybe the boss would finally notice me. Maybe I'd move up, and not have to mix paint and weigh nails all day."

"That's honest work!" said Lulu. "Nothing to be ashamed of!"

"It's not what I came to the city for."

"Quiet in the rear!"

"I thought, *Here it is. My big break.*"

"In other words, you meant to use her," said Samuel, in a voice as solemn as a judge's.

Peter Mills nodded miserably. He pushed at his glasses.

"At first," he said.

They all stared at him: Lulu, Samuel, Jenny, Theodore, and the manager with his flashlight.

"But then, she was so nice, and so pretty, and so smart, and she sort of reminded me of someone, I'm not sure. . . . She made me feel so good, the way I always used to feel back home. I always used to feel good, then."

"QUIET IN THE REAR!"

"Hey, look!" said the manager, suddenly remembering his job. "This is a real sad story. It'd make a great film. I can just see Dennis Quaid in your role. A great film. But, hey. You gotta take it someplace else, okay?"

"Dennis Quaid? Really?" Peter Mills looked a little brighter. He took off his glasses and squared his shoulders. "Dennis Quaid?"

"Yeah."

"Dennis Quaid." Peter Mills squinted. Lifting his chin, he went up the aisle and out the exit.

The manager turned his flashlight on the four children.

"I don't know how you kids got in here, but you'll have to scram. This movie's PG-Thirteen, and you two can't be over ten."

Lulu and Samuel didn't bother telling him how wrong he was. At a moment like this, being short for your age was nothing but a superficial detail.

"Come on," said Samuel. He took Theodore and Jenny,

who still clutched the enormous popcorn tub, by the hand.

In the lobby Cordelia Hill and two other girls stood looking at the posters for the coming attractions.

"Yikes! You two *again*?" she cried, just like Peter Mills. Only she wasn't horrified. She sounded tickled. "How about this time, you introduce him?"

"Ummm, this is Samuel Smith. My, uh, partner."

"Partner!" Cordelia shot looks at her two friends and they all burst into giggles.

"I'm thirsty!" said Jenny. "Want some pop, Woowoo!" She tried to drag Lulu over to the refreshment stand.

"We have to go," Lulu told Cordelia, as she and Samuel hustled the babies toward the door.

Just as they went out, Lulu heard one of the girls say, "They act like they're *married* or something!" And they all went off in another wave of giggles.

19/Cracking the Code

They'd done it! They'd revealed Peter Mills's rotten, snake-in-the-grass character! There wasn't an ounce of doubt about it now. Peter Mills was no good! Tilda was saved! Things would go back to how they used to be.

Lulu was so excited, they walked several blocks before she even wondered where they were going. By then they were near an elementary school. She spotted the ball field and Jenny spotted the playground at the same time.

"Swings, Tee-door!"

"Catch, Samuel!"

Lulu ran out onto the field. She pulled the old tennis ball out of her backpack and tossed it at Samuel. He threw up his hands as if it were a live grenade.

"I told you, I hate baseball!"

"I'll teach you. Come on, just for a couple of minutes!"

She felt so good, she had to play ball. She had to run, stretch, hurl, scoop, spin, leap—not that any of it was any fun with Samuel! He was a terrible player, the worst she'd ever seen. He looked completely mystified, even scared, as Lulu fired away at him. His throws were dribbles. He spent almost the whole time chasing the balls he missed. In his navy-blue suit and polka-dot tie he looked like something in a "What's Wrong with This Scene?" picture. If only Tilda were here! Lulu deftly scooped up a grounder, the way Tilda had taught her. When Tilda came back, day after tomorrow, what a game they'd have!

When Tilda came back, was she going to feel like playing catch?

The thought hit Lulu like a wild pitch. When Tilda came back, she was going to be all worn out from taking care of her mother. And then she was going to hear the news that her Reason for Living had forgotten she was alive.

Lulu picked up the ball and held it. Tilda wasn't going to feel like playing catch. She wasn't going to feel grateful to Lulu for saving her from Peter Mills.

She's going to feel like the whole world just slipped out from under her feet! That's how she's going to feel!

"Lulu?" Samuel called. When she didn't answer, he crossed the field. "Is the game over? I hope?"

His suit was all dusty. A lock of red-brown hair fell in his eyes. His glasses, mended with adhesive tape, sat crooked on his nose.

"I told you I'm a bad player," he said. "You shouldn't look so shocked."

"I'm thinking about my friend. The one who's in love with Peter Mills."

"Peter Mills." Samuel shook his head. "I've always despised clichés. But I can't help thinking he proves that you shouldn't judge a book by its cover."

"What do you mean?" Indignation made Lulu's ears burn and her scalp tickle. Her fury was all the greater because, deep down, she *knew* what Samuel meant.

"Maybe it was just finding out he was nearsighted. I feel an immediate sympathy for other myopic people." Samuel took off his own battered glasses and rubbed at a speck. "But I think it was more than that. When Sherry left, I thought I saw a side of him I hadn't guessed at before. He looked so—so . . ."

"Lonely," said Lulu, in spite of herself.

Samuel replaced his glasses and looked at her.

"Yes," he said. "Very, very lonely. I hope you won't be offended, Lulu. But I almost felt sorry for him."

"Ha!" Lulu crossed her arms on her chest. "He's just not used to being left out! Back home he was always the big fish."

"Not here."

"He could have been! All he had to do was let Tilda love him. All he had to do was love her back. He could've felt like a *whale*!"

"Your friend Tilda is in for a rough time," Samuel said quietly. "So are you. Breaking this news to her is going to be very difficult."

He understood. Even though he'd never met her, Samuel could see the world through Tilda's eyes.

"She taught me how to play ball," Lulu said. "I mean, I knew a little before I met her, but not much. She's the best pitcher you ever saw outside of the majors. She's got complete control, even of a knuckleball! And she spent hours giving a clodhopper like me BP. And fielding, and base running—the works! Every team she ever played on, she was voted MVP."

Samuel listened politely. Then he said, "I don't see the connection with love."

"As good as she was, she still felt like a misfit! Somehow she still felt bad about herself. She never fit in. Underneath—underneath I think she never in her whole life really expected anyone to love her."

Samuel stood very still. He looked at Lulu without speaking.

"And now I have to tell her that Peter Mills doesn't love her either. That nobody loves her, except Jenny."

"And you."

"Me!" Lulu burst out. "Some friend I am! All this time I've been following Peter Mills around and pretending I want to protect her from him—that's not the real reason! Really I just wanted to prove he was rotten and a liar because—because I wanted her to forget him! I was so jealous of him! I wasn't even thinking about her, and how bad she was going to feel when she found out the truth about him. All I was thinking about was *me.* I might as well be her enemy!"

Samuel pushed his glasses up his nose.

"It's not your fault if Peter Mills doesn't love her," he said sadly.

"He *should* love her! She's so funny, and smart, and strong! And"—Lulu thought of Tilda's voice, describing her mother—"and brave. *Real* brave. She—she's not anything like me. She's a giant and I'm just a midget beside her. In every single way." Lulu saw Samuel's brow pucker. "No offense to midgets," she said.

"I'm surprised you allowed me to accompany you on your espionage," he said stiffly. "Since you're so partial to giants."

Lulu was astonished. "I didn't mean to hurt your feelings."

Here it came. Lulu steeled herself for a blinking fit.

But instead Samuel did something she'd never seen him do before. He adjusted his glasses, drew a deep breath, and squeezed his eyes shut so tight, his jaw trembled.

Then he opened them so wide, his eyebrows disappeared up under his hair. He pointed at Lulu's backpack, lying on the trampled grass.

"I believe it's time for you to read the secret code. I told you to do it last night. Since you weren't able to, now would be the appropriate time."

Lulu walked slowly across the grass. What was it going to say? Right now, nothing would surprise her. Here she was at her moment of triumph, feeling like the world's biggest traitor. Across the playground Theodore was swinging on the only swing while Jenny patiently waited her turn. "Yahoo!" whooped Theodore. He was making more noise than Jenny. Less than a week ago he had been a grave, quiet child and Jenny had been a baby Visigoth. Everything was changed.

Life was dangerous.

"Just translate this page," said Samuel, pointing. He took a pencil, well sharpened, from the pocket of his suit jacket.

Lulu sat down. She began to work on the code. Samuel sat a few feet away from her. Out of the corner of her eye she noticed how still he was. He wasn't the kind who pulled up grass, or tossed pebbles. Perfectly still he sat, while she struggled with the secret code.

After a very long time this is what she read:

THIS IS NOT PART OF THE CASE!!!
Ice skating with you made me very happy, even though you broke my glasses. If you are wondering why I am writing this in secret code, it is because

saying it out loud would make me blink so much, it would be painful.

I would like to take you out to lunch. If you agree, please meet me at the playground tomorrow at one P.M., dressed appropriately. Jenny is cordially invited, too, of course.

Lulu stared at the page for a long time. Was that why he was all dressed up? He wanted to take her on a . . . date?

"Shoot," she said, very quietly.

Samuel cleared his throat. He waited a moment for Lulu to say something else, but when she didn't, he said, "You can tear that page out of the book. I wrote it on a separate page, you'll notice, since it doesn't have anything to do with the official investigation."

Lulu blinked. The world flickered and flared.

"You really liked ice skating with me?"

"I had never ice-skated with anyone before. I'd never . . . wanted to."

"But—"

"I told you, you can tear the page out!" he said in a desperate voice.

"I—"

"You can forget I ever wrote that! The investigation's over now, so—"

"I never could've done it without you." It was true. Now the words came tumbling out. "I would've lost my nerve every time, if you weren't there. You told me I was brave and passionate, so I tried to be, but *you're* the one. I'm just . . . shoot. I didn't even have the money for the taxi! What was I thinking of? If you hadn't come along just then, I . . ." It came to her: the money he'd spent on the taxi was the money he'd planned to spend on lunch. "And you spent all your money! Where'd you get so much money?"

"I save my allowance. I like to save money."

"So do I. I'll pay you back, as soon as I can. I mean, she's not *your* friend. You never even met her."

Once more Samuel squeezed his eyes shut, then opened them as wide as they could possibly go. "I didn't do it for her."

"Hungry hungry hungry!" Jenny and Theodore came tearing across the grass, chanting, "We want lunch lunch lunch!" (Jenny said, "wunch wunch wunch!")

Samuel looked more dismayed than ever. "For once I'm not prepared. I don't have anything! I assumed we'd go to a restaurant."

"Do you like roast beef?"

"Excuse me?"

"This is about the time my Grammie eats her Sunday dinner."

"But she's not expecting company! Especially people she never even met!"

"That's okay. She likes to feed people. Plus, she's always telling me she wants to meet my friends."

Lulu carefully closed the black notebook and put it in her backpack. She hoped Samuel would notice she didn't tear out the page.

20/Tilda Hugs the Refrigerator

The next day Cordelia Hill stopped Lulu as she headed toward her usual lunch table.

"Come sit with us. Come on! The monitors won't care!"

She nudged Lulu's tray with her own, like a sheep dog guiding a stray member of the flock. Lulu sat down across from the two girls who'd been in the theater lobby yesterday.

"How'd you like the movie yesterday?" asked Sara, who had golden ringlets tumbling to her shoulders.

"I didn't get to watch much of it," said Lulu.

"I guess not, with two babies along." She looked at Lulu as if to ask what kind of noodleheads would bring two two-year-olds along on a date.

"They didn't have the babies with them when I saw them ice skating," said Cordelia.

"He took you ice skating too?" Jessica, who was definitely wearing a bra, asked Lulu.

"On Saturday night," Cordelia answered for her. "They

met through their baby-sitting jobs. At the park, right, Lu?"

Lulu nodded. She looked down at the rice-cake-and-tahini sandwich her mother had packed for her.

"At the park," said Jessica. "That's kind of romantic, really. Kind of like in a movie. But it's a good thing for you you're so short. He's practically a dwarf."

Lulu looked up from her inedible lunch. "Superficial things don't bother us," she said.

That stunned them into silence. All three of them looked at her with—could it be?—respect. They looked at her with what possibly was even—envy.

"Here, have half my baloney," said Cordelia generously, holding out a sandwich. "The stuff your mother feeds you, it's no wonder your growth is stunted."

After school Lulu's mother picked her up and drove to the day-care center. They fetched Jenny and headed for the bus station.

Tilda wasn't even all the way off the bus before she grabbed Jenny. She swooped her up in the air, Jenny's favorite game. But Jenny's face was stony, and she said, "No, Mama! Bad Mama!"

Tilda whomped her against her chest. "You're mad at me for going away. But I couldn't help it, Shortcake." She gave Lulu and Elena a crooked smile. "My mother was right. I was worried about leaving this morning, and she said, 'Get on home. You've got your own little girl to think about.' "

She didn't say very much on the way back to Grammie's house. She sat with her legs scrunched up in the backseat, next to Jenny. She didn't have any makeup on. Lulu had only seen her without it once or twice before, and the sight made her very uneasy. Tilda looked as defenseless as a catcher without a mask.

At Grammie's house Lulu told her mother she wanted to stay for a while.

"All right," said Elena. "But be home for supper. I'm making buckwheat crêpes." She smiled at Tilda. "You'd better come, too, after you unpack. I want you fortified, so you can get back to work tomorrow. Geesh, did I ever miss you! I didn't get half the usual work done!"

"I'll make up for it tomorrow," said Tilda.

Elena drove away. Jenny marched up the front walk, still not speaking to her mother. A note on the kitchen table said Grammie had gone to get her hair done. Tilda ducked under the wagon-wheel lamp and sat at the table.

"It feels like I've been gone a couple of million years," she said. "While I was back home, shoot. It was strange. I couldn't even remember this kitchen! I tried to, and I drew a blank. I squeezed my eyes shut and all I could see was my mother's kitchen, where I grew up. All that existed was, you know. My mother and me. And now here I am back, and only a few days went by, and everything's exactly the same."

Now. Lulu pulled out a chair and sat down across from her.

"Well," she said. "Not exactly everything."

Tilda stiffened. "What?"

"I wish I never followed him around. At first I was hoping it would turn out exactly like this, but now . . ."

— 133 —

"Tell me quick."

Lulu told Tilda everything, from the first afternoon in the hardware store when Jenny chased the cat, to yesterday when Jenny bit Peter Mills on the ankle. Jenny forgot she was angry at her mother and climbed onto her lap to listen to the story.

"What—what did you say she looked like?"

"Real small, with dark hair and white skin. Kind of like a china doll."

"Doll?" asked Jenny.

Tilda nodded slowly.

"But she left him flat, right there in the movies. She's pretty but she's not a featherbrain. She could see Peter Mills for what he is. Conceited. Weak. Not to mention selfish."

"Shellfish," said Jenny.

Tilda just kept on nodding. It was a miracle how well she was taking it.

"He's not worth your little finger, Tilda."

Now Tilda shook her head, and Lulu suddenly saw the tears glinting in the corners of her eyes.

"Who could blame him?" Tilda said, and her voice began to rise. "Who could blame him, after all? He's lonesome, here in this big city. He probably thinks about home and it's like it doesn't exist anymore. He's lonesome here. Lonesome for someone to love him!"

She threw back her head and let out a wail that made Lulu's hair stand on end. Jenny stood up on her mother's lap and began to cry. She waved her fat arms, and Lulu took her. Tilda jumped out of her chair and began to pace

up and down the kitchen sobbing. Blundering into chairs
and walls, she paced back and forth like a mother lion
whose cub had disappeared. Lulu held Jenny close to
block the sight. It was terrible. It was grief on the most
monumental scale.

"Lonesome!" Tilda wailed, and she made the word
sound like the worst curse that could ever be laid on a
human being. "If only he knew. If only I could've shown
him how I loved him! I would've loved him stone blind!"

She threw her arms around the refrigerator. Grammie's
shopping list and Jenny's scribblings slipped to the floor.
This is it, thought Lulu. *This is what I hoped would happen. And now look!*

Life was so dangerous. Just twenty-four hours ago Samuel had sat in this very kitchen, eating roast beef and
mashed potatoes. His manners were impeccable. He and
Grammie had discussed the differences between Luther-
anism and Catholicism, and how to get grass stains out of
clothes. *Samuel.* Tilda hugged the refrigerator and Lulu
hugged Jenny.

"Mama!" said Jenny.

Tilda pressed her cheek against the refrigerator and
drew a long, shuddery breath. Then she turned and
reached for the baby. Jenny fastened herself to her as if
they were both made of Velcro. Tilda stroked her hair
with an enormous trembly hand.

"You've got a crazy mama, you poor little Shortcake. A
crazy mama."

"You're not crazy," said Lulu.

"Shoot! I didn't cry once the whole time I was at my

mother's. And I felt like it the whole time. Now I don't know what I'm crying over more, her or Peter."

"Don't cry over him, Tilda! He's so dumb, he doesn't even wear his glasses!"

Tilda stroked Jenny's hair. "You shouldn't talk that way about him. Don't you think I know why he liked being with me? Because I was from home! I was all primed up to worship him, just the way he was used to. Not like these people around here, who don't know he was Prom King and all that. Here he's . . . shoot. A nothing! He hates his job, he hardly knows anyone—that's the only reason he liked me. Because I—I made him feel like a big fish again."

"If you knew that, you shouldn't have fallen in love with him!"

"You're one hundred percent right." Tilda rocked from foot to foot. Jenny was falling asleep on her shoulder. "I should've listened to you all along. You tried to warn me off him from the first."

Lulu's ears burned. Even though things could never again be the same between her and Tilda, she didn't want to start lying to her now.

"That was just because I was jealous," she said.

Tilda nodded calmly. She didn't look the least bit surprised by the revelation. "You don't have to tell me about jealousy. I've been jealous of people my whole life. But it's a snake pit. Poor Peter. He might feel as bad as I do, right now. Having Snow White II walk out on him. That must have knocked his socks clean off."

Lulu remembered Peter, standing in the aisle of the

movie theater, his glasses slipping down his perfect nose, his nearsighted eyes squinting at the EXIT sign. Looking as if he'd just been sent back to the farm team, for good.

"Maybe you're right," said Lulu. "But he still thinks he looks like Dennis Quaid."

Tilda shook her head. She stroked Jenny's hair and looked out the window over the sink.

"Going home, I learned a lot. Too much, for such a few days. It's still all boiling over inside me, but . . . well. I know everybody needs love. Every single body, whether they act like it or not. Whether they want to or not."

She stared out the window. Jenny was asleep on her shoulder.

Lulu tugged her cap down and thought about what Tilda had said. The Tilda who had left home four days ago would have wanted Peter Mills skinned alive. Tilda had learned things while she was gone. Things about love. Things about herself.

Me, too, maybe.

When Lulu looked up, Tilda was smiling down at her.

"Hey," she said, the tears still shining in her eyes. She pushed Lulu's cap back on her head. "Who's this Samuel guy, anyway?"

21/Ready, Set . . .

The workout was more strenuous than ever. Tilda made
Lulu run laps, sprint, and swing three bats at once. Lulu's
legs buckled and her arms were ready to fall off. It was
wonderful. When Tilda fired home a fastball, and Lulu
managed to catch it and keep it, it was just like the old
days. Her hand was a cinder. She was covered with sweat.
Tilda grinned, acknowledging the play.

We're connected.

But already it was getting dark, and when Tilda tried to
demonstrate her knuckleball the pitches kept sinking. It
was too cold. A few minutes after they stopped playing,
Lulu began to feel it. They wouldn't stop at Baskin-Robbins tonight. As they trudged back to Grammie's, Lulu
began to think of cocoa. She imagined the two of them at
Grammie's kitchen table, beneath the yellow light of the
wagon wheel, blowing across their mugs. Jenny, in her
pink flannel sleeper, would climb into Lulu's lap and beg
for cocoa too. It was Friday night. They could stay up late.
Maybe Lulu could even sleep over, and—

"Lu." Tilda's voice came sharp and sudden as the cold

night air. "Can you . . . would you, you know . . . Shoot. Could you baby-sit for me tonight?"

Lulu stumbled, but Tilda caught her before she hit the sidewalk.

"Baby-sit? You mean you're . . . going out?"

Tilda rubbed her ear with her palm. As they passed beneath a streetlamp, Lulu saw that her hair was stringy and her makeup smudged.

"A . . . you know. A friend of mine is coming by in a little while. We're going to get pizza together. Or something."

Friend? The word wasn't a part of Tilda's working vocabulary. If she was going out with a friend, though, it had to be a girl. Tilda was a sweaty, smudgy, stringy mess. It would take her hours to look as good as she used to look for Duck Eyes.

Peter Mills had called her once, almost two weeks ago. Lulu was there, in Grammie's kitchen, when he did. She heard Tilda tell him politely, "No. Thanks anyway."

There was a pause, where she leaned against the refrigerator and her brow wrinkled just like Jenny's when something broke her heart. Then Tilda suddenly stood up straight, and started telling Peter how things were these days in their hometown. He must have been interested. Tilda talked for a long time, and he hardly interrupted at all. At the end of the conversation she told him she'd be going home pretty often, so she could fill him in on the hometown news, if he wanted. She'd probably see him at the hardware store sometime. When she hung up she looked desolate, but not demented, for quite a while. Then she asked Lulu if she was ready for a practice.

Tilda hadn't mentioned him since. Since then all she'd done was work hard for Elena, play with Jenny, call her mother every night, and practice with Lulu. Things were almost the way they used to be—except that every afternoon, Lulu met Samuel at the park. Since the official investigation had ended, it was the only place they met. Samuel hadn't mentioned the word *date* again. They just stood or sat, watching the babies play, stuffing their hands in their pockets to keep warm. Samuel always brought an ample supply of tissues. Neither of them speculated on what they'd do when it finally got too cold to spend afternoons there.

Tilda wanted to meet Samuel. She pestered Lulu about it all the time. She wanted to meet Theodore too. She and Grammie had both noticed that Jenny was acting much more civilized lately. Grammie said it must be her having him for a friend that made the difference. "She's starting to realize she's not the sun at the center of the universe. She's catching on to the idea that other folks' feelings are important too." That, said Tilda, was possibly the biggest lesson Jenny would ever learn in her entire life.

But Lulu still hadn't introduced them. She was afraid Tilda would peer down at Samuel in a way that would bring on a horrendous blinking fit. And she was sure Samuel would act his stiffest and most formal, making Tilda roll her eyes as if to ask, *Who starched your underwear?* making Samuel blink even harder. It would be a disaster. A tragedy, even.

Still, her heart sank at the thought of her two best friends never meeting and liking each other.

Two best friends? *Two* best friends?

"You're not saying anything," said Tilda. "Does that mean you can't baby-sit? Or . . . you won't?"

"Could I just ask one thing?"

"What?"

"What's your—your friend's name?"

"Ralph."

Ralph? Could it possibly be a girl's name? Short for Ralphina?

"He hates it. He says it makes him sound like the kind of guy who kicks puppies and eats raw meat." Tilda slid Lulu a look. "I told him I have another good friend who hates her name too."

So it was true. Lulu swallowed. Tilda was going on another date. She was falling in love.

It was starting *all over again.*

Only, this time there was no emerald-green or flaming-crimson dress. No tearing of hair or spending of entire paychecks. This time there was only Tilda in her baggy sweats, calmly describing someone who hated his name.

"I met him in the library, that day your mother sent me for a book on building arches. He was shelving books. He works at the library part time and goes to the community college. He said, 'You never built an arch before? You're just going to look it up in a book and see what happens?' And I said, 'What's the point of living if you don't take a few risks?' And he started, you know. Laughing, and—"

"Does he drive too fast?"

"What?"

"Like Peter Mills."

Tilda snorted. "I don't even know if he has a car. He's just a poor student."

"Does he look like an ad for perfume?"

"When he called me up last night, I knew his voice right away. But I just got a blur on his face. That's the kind of looks he has. I do remember he's shorter than me. That really got me. The whole time we were talking he was craning his neck and it didn't seem to, you know. Bother him a titch. I told him I have another good friend who's kind of short too."

Now Tilda smiled, and Lulu saw that beneath her calmness she was, after all, excited. It was a different kind of excitement from what she'd felt for Peter Mills, but it was there.

"He lives with his father. His mother's dead. We talked about, you know. Hospitals."

They must have talked for a long time. You didn't meet someone and immediately say, "By the way, if there's one thing I hate it's a hospital. How about you?"

"I know I shouldn't have waited till the last minute to ask you to baby-sit. But, well, you know. Will you?"

"Okay," said Lulu.

Tilda threw an arm around her shoulder and squeezed her together like an accordion.

At Grammie's house Tilda went upstairs to take a shower. Lulu sat at the kitchen table, watching Grammie cook and Jenny bang pots around on the floor. She was telling them they were good pots and she loved them.

Demented.

Lulu felt the sweat from their practice drying on her skin, and she knew she should take a shower too. But she couldn't move. She sat there at the table, waiting for it to hit her.

Peter Mills hadn't gotten love out of Tilda's system. Nothing was going to get it out. As badly as Peter Mills had hurt her, Tilda was ready to give her heart away again. She was always going to want something Lulu would never be able to give her.

"Your name Tee-door," Jenny told the colander. "Samwell," she called the grater.

In spite of herself Lulu smiled. Then she waited for the sadness to hit her.

But before that could happen, the telephone rang.

"Oh, hello," said Grammie, in a pleased voice. "Fine, thank you. A little touch of the arthritis, with this cold setting in, but— Is that so! Potato water? I never heard that remedy before. . . . *Your* granny? That's good enough for me. . . . You sure can, dear! She's sitting right here." Grammie held out the receiver to Lulu.

"Samuel?"

"Hello, Lulu."

They had never talked on the phone before. His voice didn't sound as deep as in person. Instead, it sounded almost thin as he said, "I called you at home, but your mother gave me Grammie's number."

"You talked to my *mother*?"

"At some length. In fact, I think it was the longest

phone conversation of my life. I don't usually like to talk on the phone."

But you called me.

"I don't either."

"Your mother seemed to require my entire biography."

"I'm sorry. That's just how she is."

"I might still be on the phone with her if Theodore hadn't somehow managed to put an entire roll of paper down the, uh, ahem. Toilet. My mother says his inventiveness these days astonishes her. She asks him, 'Who's been teaching you this mischief, little man?' Anyway, when the water began to seep from the bathroom into the kitchen, it provided a suitable excuse to hang up on your mother. Politely, of course."

He cleared his throat. Lulu could imagine him adjusting his glasses, which he'd had repaired. She could almost smell Dreft.

"I was calling with a suggestion," he said. "Tomorrow afternoon my parents are going to work at our church, and I have to baby-sit. The Accu-Weather forecast is for cold rain. Would you and Jenny like to come over?"

"You mean . . ."

"The babies could play, and we could commence your chess lessons." Lulu could almost hear him blinking. "That is, of course, unless you already have other plans, or if you just don't want to, I will understand, since I hate baseball. But I thought I'd put the idea on the table. My parents have already given their approval. But if you don't—"

"I'd like it a lot."

"Excuse me?"

"Coming over, I mean. I don't know about chess."

"I had one other thing to tell you. I hope you don't mind if I relay it in secret code."

"Wait till I get a pencil. Okay."

"Here it is: RG RH KLHHRYOV GSZG BLF SZEV XSZMTVW NB ORJV R YVORVEV JFIGSVI RMEVHGRTZGRLM RH MVXVHHZIB. Have you got it?"

"Yes."

"Good." Samuel sputtered out his address and hung up.

Lulu stared down at the secret code for a long time. Then, working slowly and carefully, she deciphered it. She checked it over three times, to make sure that was really what it said. Sitting back in her chair, she imagined Samuel sitting in *his* kitchen, his kitchen where she would be tomorrow, learning a game that was a complete mystery to her, while the babies made mischief and the cold rain slanted against the windows. . . .

"Are you sure you're ready for this?"

Tilda stood in the kitchen doorway. She had changed into clean jeans and a T-shirt, and swept her hair back in a barrette. She wore makeup, but not much. Her collarbone stuck out. In her shiny pink ears the diamond hearts (they looked real, even if they weren't) seemed to shine brighter than ever before.

"Are you sure you're ready, Lu?"

Lulu knew she didn't mean ready for baby-sitting. She meant ready for Ralph, for the possibility everything would change all over again, for all of dangerous, unpredictable, real life.

Sitting in the yellow kitchen light, Lulu pushed her cap back from her brow. And then the doorbell rang. Grammie turned from the stove. Jenny hugged her colander. Tilda shuddered from head to toe.

"I'll get it," Lulu said. Standing up, she gave one of her two best friends a punch in the shoulder.

"I'm ready," she said.

And heading down the hallway, she knew she was.

About the Author

Tricia Springstubb is the author of numerous short stories, picture books, and young adult novels, including *Give and Take* and *The Moon on a String;* a trilogy, *Which Way to the Nearest Wilderness?, Eunice Gottlieb and the Unwhitewashed Truth About Life,* and *Eunice (the Egg Salad) Gottlieb,* as well as another book about Lulu: *With a Name Like Lulu, Who Needs More Trouble?*

Tricia Springstubb lives in Cleveland Heights, Ohio, with her husband and three children, Zoe, Phoebe, and Delia.